THE TOFF'S MISTAKE

was that he didn't take Daffodil
seriously. The blonde young artist
looked like a brainless sexpot, but
she had a temper—and a secret. Before
the secret was out, Daff had disappeared,
the Toff was embroiled with four
unpredictable and dangerous girls,
Mme. Tussaud's wax museum was in
an uproar—and Death waited to
take the last trick in the game. . . .

200,000
4 800,000

THE TOFF
IN WAX

JOHN CREASEY

▲

PYRAMID BOOKS • **NEW YORK**

AUTHOR'S NOTE

I am most grateful to the management and staff at Madame Tussaud's, particularly to Mr. Bernard Tussaud and Mr. James Catney, who not only gave me a great deal of help most courteously, but also allowed me all the licence an author could possibly need to make an Exhibition of such renown fit his history. All the other characters are entirely fictitious.

JOHN CREASEY

THE TOFF IN WAX

A PYRAMID BOOK

Published by arrangement with Walker and Company

Walker and Company edition published April, 1966
Pyramid edition published May, 1968

Library of Congress Catalog Card Number: 66-16922

Printed in the United States of America

PYRAMID BOOKS are published by Pyramid Publications, Inc., 444 Madison Avenue, New York, New York 10022, U.S.A.

CONTENTS

CHAPTER 1

MISTAKES BY THE TOFF

ROLLISON felt the pressure on his chest, and sudden, hot pressure on his face. He was blinded and he could not see, he was gasping yet he could not breathe through the tiny tubes. In those few awful seconds he feared that he had been fooled, that these men and the girl meant to kill him—to suffocate him. Hands pressed against the warm clay on his face, into his eyes, his mouth, his nostrils. The world grew dark; as black as death.

Suddenly, blindingly, he thought: They're not from Tussaud's.

As suddenly, a man said: "Half-a-jiff—just hold your breath."

He felt as if he had no breath to hold, but at least the fear subsided. He did not know how long the 'half-a-jiff' really lasted, but it seemed a long, long time. He was beginning to heave and the band about his chest was like steel, when the man spoke again.

"Here we are, sir! All over and done with!"

The pressure lifted. Light crept in to ease the darkness, and Rollison could breathe. Above him, a little podge of a man beamed down on him, red-faced, bright-eyed. In both hands he held a half-sphere of waxy-looking clay, as if an odd-shaped ball had been cut in two.

"Got you all in there—perfect likeness, that will be."

Rollison grunted.

"And before you can say knife you'll be in the Chamber of Horrors," the podge declared brightly. "Can't say we've got many detectives in the Exhibition, but we've got a few toffs. Ha-ha-ha!"

The Honorable Richard Rollison, known to so many as the Toff, was only just beginning to get his breath back, and was in no mood to appreciate such witticisms. So he grunted, and concentrated on deep breathing. A rare and remarkable thing happened almost at that moment. An attractive girl drew near him, and he did not notice her.

"There's only one Toff," she declared. "Isn't there, Mr. Rollison?"

He turned towards the sound of her voice. It was a nice voice, but not as exceptional as her face and hair. In a quick judgment she might have been thought beautiful, but her nose was a trifle too short, and her lips too full. No one could possibly question the beauty of her eyes, which were hazel-coloured or honey-coloured—one could take one's choce—or of the golden sheen of her hair.

"I'll go this far with you," Rollison said. "There's only one me."

"That won't last for long," interpolated the podgy man, whose name was Wilberforce. "Soon be a pair of you. Funny time of life to become a twin, isn't it? Like being born again."

"But I doubt if Mr. Rollison wants to be born again," said the girl.

It looked as if the sun had been caught in her hair and her eyes, and was still trapped in the pale, almost lustrous gold of her skin, and yet her voice, her manner, what she said and how she said it were all sombre if not ominous.

"Do you?" she asked him.

"Don't be silly, Daff," Wilberforce said. He appeared to have stopped seeing the funny side of the situation. Something the girl had said had punctured his bright mood, and he placed the half-sphere, which was a cast of Rollison's face, carefully on a sheet of tissue paper spread over a small table. "I was only joking."

"And weren't you only joking?" Rollison asked the girl called Daff.

"Guess," she said.

"No," said the Toff.

"No what?"

"You were not joking."

"Would you like to be born again?"

"Now, Daff," podgy Wilberforce protested earnestly, "that's heresy, that is."

"You might squeeze it into sacrilegious, but it's not remotely heretical," the girl declared. "Even sacrilegious would be putting too fine a point on it. Don't you think so, Mr. Rollison?"

"I do indeed," the Toff agreed.

Daff almost smiled, sufficient to make it obvious that a full, true smile from her would create radiance.

"Taken by and large, and assuming you mean physically and not spiritually, I would not like to be born again," Rollison stated simply. "What does that make me?"

"Exactly what you are," declared Daff: and she turned away.

That was the moment when Rollison made his first avoidable mistake. It was born out of kindliness, and in fact of admiration, but also—and perhaps mostly—out of nostalgia for his own youth. The girl was twenty-two or three, he guessed, and that made her very young by his no means dotage standards. He did not want to end this unlikely conversation on a sour, or even an unfriendly note, so he spoke in a tone which was calculated to make her relent.

"Now, Daphne," he said. "Don't you think we could—"

She startled him by spinning round; almost by pirouetting. He had not noticed how lithe she was, how beautifully her body moved; and to do him justice he had not realised how little she wore beneath her pearl grey sweater and her tight black skirt. Everything danced as she swung round, even her golden-coloured hair, and especially her bosom: her lips seemed to quiver, too.

"My name's not Daphne! Oh, you're insufferable!"

She glared at him, and as she did so, Wilberforce—who had effaced himself with either shame or embarrassment—made a sighing sound.

"Now, Daff," he protested.

He stopped his half-hearted wrapping of the Toff's cast in tissue paper, and stared appealingly across the table at Daff whose name was not Daphne. It was doubtful whether the girl heard or noticed him, she was so enraged by what Rollison had said. In a far corner, a tall, spindly, melancholy man was packing tools and clay and gauze; he appeared to be oblivious of the situation between Rollison and the girl.

Then Rollison made his second mistake; he smiled. Perhaps the smile was too broad; perhaps it suggested a kind of condescension, or even avuncular or parental long-sufferance. Whatever the reason, it made Daff suddenly, furiously, beautifully angry. Her eyes sparked and her colour glowed and her hands rose; for a moment Rollison thought she was going to strike him.

"Daff!" cried podgy Wilberforce.

Daff glared and glowered, then swung round again with the same tantalising glory, and strode out of the room. From behind, too, she was a remarkable sight.

At the door, hovering, was Rollison's man Jolly. He showed himself sufficiently to let Rollison know that he was on duty.

There was a flurry of footsteps and the sound of a door opening, followed by Jolly's mild and deferential voice.

"Good afternoon, Miss."

If Jolly spoke like that in the hope of sparking the girl to another outburst, he failed. The front door closed. Wilberforce, a man of some five feet four, with thin fair hair and a chin and a nose almost buried in fat, turned away from the door towards Rollison.

"Oh, I *am* sorry," he said.

"I don't see why you should be." Rollison swung himself off the trestle table, imported into his living-room-cum-study for the making of the cast, and sat with his legs dangling. He had forgotten the physical discomfort of a few minutes ago.

"Well," said Wilberforce, "I feel kind of responsible."

"That's a lot to be responsible for," remarked Rollison. "Will she work on the mask?"

"Yes. On the make-up and the colouring."

"Oh," said Rollison. "I shall probably look like a cross between a sufferer from yellow jaundice and a ghoul."

"Oh, she won't take it out on your model!"

"Only on me?"

"Try to forget her," pleaded Wilberforce. "She's been a bit upset about something this last day or so."

"I'm not sure that I want to forget her," objected Rollison.

"Now, please, Mr. Rollison—don't take it personally. She's the same with everyone lately. She's got a bee in her bonnet, that's all there is to it. She'll make a very good job of you, you can be sure of that."

"I suppose that's something to be thankful for," conceded Rollison. He smiled, and turned to the cast. "Are you sure that will be all right?"

"Perfect likeness, sir, even to the eyelashes," answered the podge. "My new wax-clay method may be a bit uncomfortable, but it never fails, and it saves a lot of time. You'll be standing up there as large as life in a week or two." He was fast recovering from his perturbation as he picked up the big ball of tissue paper and placed it, almost with reverence, into a square cardboard box. "No offence taken, I hope, sir." Wilberforce placed the lid on the box and twisted two wooden clips, which kept the lid in position. Then he leaned across to Rollison, and went on with a conspiratorial air. "You won't complain, sir?"

"Complain to whom?"

"The boss—Mr. Bernard."

"What about?" asked Rollison obtusely. And then he laughed. "Oh, about Daff."

"No other cause for complaint, sir, have you?"

"I won't know until I've seen what my twin looks like," replied Rollison.

Wilberforce stared; then frowned; then suddenly saw the joke. He burst out into a guffaw of laughter which made every surplus ounce of flab on his body quiver. He was still chuckling in fits and starts when at last he went towards the door. A step behind him went the tall melancholy man who had prepared the waxy clay. Jolly, hovering at another door, realised that Rollison was going to see the craftsmen out, so he moved from sight. Rollison opened the front door, and on a chorus of goodbyes the two men reached the top of the steps which served 22a Gresham Terrace.

Suddenly, Rollison exclaimed: "Just a minute!"

The podge stopped and the long lean man collided with him.

"Did you call, sir?"

"Yes. If her name isn't Daphne, what is it?"

"Daffodil," answered Wilberforce. "Isn't it pretty, sir?"

Yes, thought Rollison, Daffodil was pretty as far as it went, but it would not necessarily appeal to its possessor. In fact the Daff he knew might well resent the fact that she had been named after Spring's most poem'd flower. Daffodil. It suited her colouring and her hair, too, if not her mood. Musing thus, Rollison took his ease in an armchair in the room now cleared of the trestle table, and looking its proper and distinguished self again. There was Rollison's large pedestal desk, made of finely figured walnut, the rich Indian carpet from Mirzapore, the bookcases with the bottom sections turned into filing cabinets, the armchairs deep in comfort, the television set, the corner cupboard which concealed a bar of infinite variety.

And there was the Trophy Wall.

Those few who came into this room ignorant of Rollison's reputation always stopped in front of the wall, and gaped or gasped or did not believe their eyes. For on display was a collection of lethal weapons more fitting to a macabre museum of murder. In fact it was a museum to all intents and purposes, beautifully set out and catalogued. There for all who dared to go close were cards showing who had been killed by any particular weapon, and who the killer had been.

There was one other thing which the exhibits on this wall had in common. In every case, the Honourable Richard Rollison had caught the killer. Hence his fame (or as he preferred to call it, his notoriety). And hence the fact that he was to be on show, in wax, at Madame Tussaud's famed exhibition. For the most sensational murder in a decade, Charles Adam Franken and his wife were also going into the Exhibition. Charles Adam Franken and his wife had killed an elderly relative, and later a policeman. Rollison had actually caught them.

"I was lucky," the Toff would say.

Lucky or not, he was to keep the Frankens company at Madame Tussaud's.

Rollison was not a particularly vain man, but this mark of distinction both amused and pleased him. From the day his effigy first appeared, he would be the victim of unending leg-pulling, but none he hoped with malice.

He drowsed, speculating idly about Daffodil. He was seldom idle, but this afternoon's appointment had made him cancel an engagement with the committee of the Juvenile Delinquency Inquiry, and he had not been sure how long the cast-taking would take. It was one of those lulls between cases, too; he had been told that even the police were quiet. The hot weather must be encouraging many criminals to rest.

Jolly came in, with tea on a silver tray, wafer-thin bread and butter and a single chocolate éclair. He placed this at Rollison's side, and stood back. He was a man of medium height, who looked short, rather sad and at times almost woebegone. In fact he was alert and lively at nearly sixty-five. He had served the Toff for thirty years, and looked good for thirty more.

"Bring another cup, and sit down," said Rollison, and when Jolly returned with a cup and saucer and a plate with another éclair, Rollison went on: "What did you make of her, Jolly?"

"A somewhat tempestuous young woman, sir."

"And what?"

"Like so many, I fear, quite spoiled."

"Happy, do you think?"

"I was of the opinion, sir, that she was likely to be happy only when she was unhappy."

"I'm not sure that I think you're right," Rollison said.

"Spoiled? Or hurt? Tempestuous? Or troubled? What are the odds against my ever finding out?"

"About ten to one on, if you become really interested," said Jolly drily.

"But you don't see why I should," remarked Rollison.

There is no way of telling, but it is doubtful whether he would have taken sufficient interest to learn more about Daffodil, had there not been an unexpected sequel to the cast-taking of that afternoon. He did not hear about it until the next morning, just after ten o'clock, when he was at his desk pondering a Prison Visit, due that day, to see one of the most incorrigible criminals of the age. How did one help those who wished for no help?

"Rollison," he said into the telephone.

"Mr. Rollison," a man said, and it was immediately obvious that he was labouring under the stress of some emotion. "It's Jim Catlin here, of Madame Tussaud's. I hardly know how to say this, I've never had to say anything like it before." He paused, and breathed deeply, and went on: "That cast we took yesterday has been disfigured sir, sir. Someone has burnt out one eye."

CHAPTER 2

A HOLE IN THE EYE

"MR. ROLLISON," said Catlin. "I can't tell you how distressed I am. It's a shocking thing to have happened."

"Don't rate it too high," said Rollison. "It's only a hole in a piece of clay. Do you know when it happened?"

"Unfortunately, no. That is, not with any precision. It was in perfect order at half-past six last night. I examined it myself with Wilberforce."

"Wilberforce?"

"Surely you know—the modeller, the man who made the cast."

"Oh, yes, of course. You both saw it at half-past six, you say." Rollison paused. "I suppose you actually looked inside."

"Oh, there's no doubt at all." Catlin was not exactly indignant, but in different circumstances he probably would have been. He was a young man of medium height, dark, well-dressed, just now a little over-earnest, certainly not overawed. He sat at his desk in an office behind the Exhibition Rooms, an hour after he had telephoned Rollison. On the walls were photographs of famous men and women, all autographed, all taken by Catlin, who was curator, public relations officer and photographer-in-chief to Madame Tussaud's. The office windows were closed and there was a faint hum of air-conditioning. Catlin continued: "Wilberforce unwrapped the cast, and we looked into the concave mirror which we use to check for blemishes. They seldom happen with the new process, but they can. Would you like to come across to the workshop? I can show you everything then."

"I'd like to very much," said Rollison. "May I ask one or two questions first?"

"Why, certainly."

"When was the damage discovered?"

"Just about nine o'clock this morning."

"Who by?"

"Oh, Wilberforce. He did another check."

"Is that customary?"

"Invariably. More habit that precaution, I would say."

"I see. Who did it?"

Catlin looked blank, as if he had not heard the question.

"I beg your pardon?"

"Who burned the hole in the wax?" asked Rollison more precisely.

"I only wish we knew!"

"Have you any idea at all?"

"If I had, he or she would have been instantly dismissed."

"You mean that it couldn't have happened by accident?"

"That would be quite impossible. Mr. Rollison," asserted Catlin, leaning forward over the desk, "the damage was done quite deliberately. Wilful damage—to *you*."

Rollison said mildly: "Why me?"

"But it's *your* face!"

"It's your property and will cost you time and money."

"You mean—" Catlin gave a strained kind of laugh, and placed his hands on the desk in front of him. His fingernails were beautifully kept, his hands were soft and and pale in colour. "You mean, did someone do it to annoy or to injure Madame Tussaud's? Most certainly not, sir."

"What makes you so sure?"

"There were hundreds—thousands!—of poundsworth of valuable waxwork within easy reach. New models almost finished, some just started, several casts, a great deal of beeswax, and other raw material. Oh no, Mr. Rollison, that damage was wilful, and it was directed against you and no one else."

"It seems likely," admitted the Toff. He felt a little shiver go through him, not exactly of apprehension or of fear, but not far removed from either.

Why should anyone do such a thing? There were several answers, none of which he wanted to accept at this stage.

"Between the hours of six-thirty last evening and nine o'clock this morning, some ill-wisher broke in, burned the hole in your eye, and left unseen." The fact that Catlin gave the words a touch of melodrama did not affect their vividness; in fact it heightened it."

"Were there any signs of breaking in?" asked Rollison.

"None."

"So a key was used," said Rollison, without thinking.

"Does that necessarily follow? Could not entry be forced without a trace?"

"I shouldn't think so," Rollison reasoned. "The police would have a lot more problems on their hands if that kind of entry was easy." He leaned back in his chair. "What about suspects?"

"There are no suspects."

"Oh," said Rollison. "None at all?"

"You speak as if you thought there were," Catlin said, and this time he was very nearly indignant.

Two things passed through Rollison's mind. First, that if this man really suspected no one, he had not been told of the curious behaviour of Daffodil at the time of casting. Second, that Catlin was being a little too emphatic, almost as if he did indeed have suspicions but preferred not to say so.

Rollison smiled as he stood up.

"I hoped there would be," he said, almost flatly. "Shall we go and see the workshop?"

"By all means," said Catlin, and sprang to his feet. "It's not far away—quite close, in fact. We can go the back way."

The back way was up a flight of narrow stairs, past two open doors through which Rollison caught a glimpse of

robed wax fiures, and floodlighting. They looked out on to
a cobbled yard, crammed with small cars and motor-
scooters. This led into a turning which in turn led to the
bustle of Baker Street, near the dome of the Planetarium,
which reminded Rollison of the half-sphere of his damaged
cast.

Catlin walked with almost nervous haste until they
reached a small landing.

"Down here," he said.

He stepped beyond some open double doors and into a
big workshop, brightly lit by fluorescent strip. On one side
was a bench, like a huge laboratory bench; on the other
were wax figures, draped and undraped, big and small,
pallid and flamboyant. At least twenty people were working at various stages of shaping and altering and dressing
and padding. One section of the bench was filled with
wigs and toupees, of all colours, kinds and sizes, men's
and women's, boys' and girls'. Beyond this was a theatrical
dresser's mirror, the mirror framed in lights. In most of
the mirror was a statue of a man, wearing shoes and
trousers, but nothing else. By the side of the figure Daffodil stood and peered into the reflection of the face, until
suddenly she moved forward and rubbed pink into the
white wax cheeks.

Catlin had nodded to some others as they had passed,
but had not gone out of his way to speak or to look at
them. Now he paused.

" 'Morning, Daff."

Daffodil looked up.

"Good morning," she said. There was no great warmth
in her voice nor in her expression, but it was white heat
compared with the way she looked when she recognised
Rollison.

"Good morning," Rollison said pleasantly.

"How's our latest murderer?" inquired Catlin with a
forced jocularity which would have done credit to the
podge. The question caused the girl no surprise or embarrassment. She looked over Rollison's head as she answered.

"He'll be ready for tomorrow."

"Good girl," said Catlin. He examined the face of the
figure of a man whom Rollison now recognised; he had
been hanged a few days earlier, for the murder of a policeman. "Not too much red on the lips," Catlin advised.
"He had pale lips."

"I know what his lips were like," Daffodil said icily.

"Yes, of course. Just a reminder." Catlin gave her a quick, almost nervous smile, then rejoined Rollison. "Very clever young artist," he remarked. "Temperamental, though. All good artists are, I suppose. Now—here are the modelling rooms."

He led the way through a wide sliding door into a narrow passage with doors to the right and left. He went into the second. It was like a small laboratory, with all the scientific paraphernalia, most of the apparatus familiar to any layman, such as bell jars and pipettes, Bunsen burners and test tubes, crucibles and microscopes. Along one wall were shelves on which stood dozens of bottles, containing powders and liquids of many colours. On the opposite wall were dozens of face masks, masks of wax and clay and plaster, two or three of bronze.

Every face was familiar. They ranged from politician to sportsman. Beatle to opera singer, judge to criminal. It was like being stared at by a gallery of the living and the dead, the good and the bad.

Beneath this wall stood Wilberforce. He seemed to take on the hue of wax, pale whitish-grey in colour, and that made his little, buried eyes startlingly blue. His white smock, spotlessly clean for the occasion, made him seem even more podgy, and he was nervous as he looked at Rollison.

"I—er—I can't tell you how upset I am, Mr. Rollison. This is a terrible thing to have happened—terrible."

Wilberforce turned to his bench and picked up the cast which he had put away with such care at the Gresham Terrace flat. There were no signs of damage until he turned it upside down. Then a hole about the size of a pullet's egg showed. The edges were rimmed with off-white wax, but the shape was almost perfect.

"The shape of an *eye*," breathed Wilberforce.

And so it was.

Rollison drew closer.

"How was it done?" he asked.

"There is only one possible method," answered the podge. "A hot stone or hard object was put inside, in this way." He placed the cast on the bench, open side upwards, the round section resting between two pieces of wood, so that nothing actually touched the waxy clay. Next, he picked up a pair of tweezers, or tongs, like those used for washing machines but of a much better quality wood. With these, he picked up what looked like an oval-shaped marble, and with great care placed it inside the cast.

It fell through, and rolled on the bench.

"That was precisely how it was done. I imagine that the object used was heated over a Bunsen burner until it became hot enough to melt the clay around the eye. I use a kind of wax which hardens quickly, until it is almost like clay. If you come closer"—Wilberforce moved so that Rollison could draw near, and peer inside the cast—"you will see that the hole inside is much larger—more clay melted when the object was first placed inside."

Rollison saw how right he was; and shivered.

"Very ugly, sir," agreed Wilberforce solemnly.

"Hideous," muttered Catlin. "To burn out your eyes."

Only then did it begin to dawn on Rollison that to these men, mask and a cast had life and character, perhaps even feeling of its own. It was as if a human being had been disfigured in this beastly way.

"And you've no idea who did it," Rollison said softly.

"I keep telling you—no." Catlin was sharp-voiced.

Wilberforce didn't speak, but peered almost pleadingly into Rollison's eyes; he could not have asked Rollison more clearly not to press this question. So Rollison went on:

"It must have been someone who knows the place."

"Hundreds do," said Catlin.

"People come in and out," Wilberforce declared almost eagerly. "Special visitors to the Exhibition, people from all over the world come here. This new method of casting has attracted a great deal of interest from many quarters, hasn't it, Mr. Catlin?"

"A very great deal."

"And we have the secret, the know-how . . ."

"Don't be modest," Catlin reproved. "Wilberforce invented this, Mr. Rollison. It saves a lot of time and money—and more and more waxwork exhibitions are being opened all over the world. We have the opportunity of considerable export trade in masks and casts and even figures, even though we have never made a model for anyone else. However, hundreds of experts come through the workshops most weeks. Don't they, Wilberforce?"

"And they're most welcome," Wilberforce declared.

"Naturally."

"But one of them did this," remarked Rollison.

"Of course!" insisted Catlin. "Who else would?"

It would have been easy for Rollison to point out that the vandal must have known how to break in, known his way about the labyrinthine passages, found this room, identified the cast, been competent in the use of the Bunsen burner. He said nothing of these things, but put his hand beneath the cast, touched the oval-shaped marble, which was cold to his skin, and picked it up.

It was a glass eye, with a honey-coloured iris; the same colour as Daffodil's eyes.

"Was that used?" Rollison asked.

"Possibly," conceded Wilberforce.

"We can't hope to be sure," insisted Catlin.

He was very anxious to throw doubt on the possibility that an employee had done this thing; over-anxious, in fact. At the same time he obviously took a very grave view. Both men stood watching Rollison, as if afraid of what he would say next. He wanted time to reflect on the oddness of their behaviour as well as of what had happened, so he stalled.

"What are you going to do?" he asked.

"What *are* we to do?" asked Catlin.

"Obviously your premises were burgled."

"You mean—we should tell the police?"

"Don't you want to?"

"Mr. Rollison, it would inevitably lead to publicity of the most unwanted kind. Don't you see that?"

"The police would treat it as confidential."

"The story would be bound to leak out. Such a personage as you—"

"Do you want to report it to the police?" Wilberforce asked in a high-pitched voice.

"Not particularly," Rollison answered. "I haven't suffered personally." He nearly added: "Yet."

"Then we won't, either. We will assume that it was a piece of malicious damage which can be overlooked," Catlin said. "There is one other thing."

"Yes?"

"Will you consent to having a second cast taken?"

"Yes," said Rollison promptly.

"You're very kind, and you can be sure we appreciate it. When do you think would be convenient for you?" Catlin asked.

"Why not now?" asked Rollison.

The eyes of both men lit up.

The process was exactly the same as it had been at Rollison's flat, but Daffodil was not present. The lean and melancholy man was. No one spoke to him and he spoke to no one, just went about his task of preparing the waxy clay by warming, and adjusting the bench on which Rollison was to lie. The bench, rather like a doctor's couch, was in one of the small rooms near Wilberforce's workshop.

"We prefer clients to be in their own homes, we find they are more relaxed," Wilberforce said. "Not that we need ever fear that you won't be relaxed, Mr. Rollison. Now—on your back, please . . . Excellent . . . You know exactly what to expect, don't you? . . . Very good . . . It will only last a few seconds. I know it seems much longer but in fact it isn't . . . *Now*."

He poked two short straws into Rollison's nostrils, so that Rollison could breathe, then placed the warm, pliable stuff on Rollison's face. It was like having a wad of dough, rolled out on the pastry board, slapped over one's face and pressed down. Rollison had exactly the same reactions as on the first occasion, the sense of pressure, of suffocation, of fear, and he also had a strange sensation of burning at his left eye. He knew that this was imagination, that there was nothing to fear, but he wanted to shout and struggle, flinging the warm, moist stuff off.

"Here we are, sir! All over and done with." Wilberforce's voice sounded exactly the same as it had yesterday. The pressure eased, light spread through the blackness, and the podgy face, red and merry-looking, was just above him.

"Got you all in there! Perfect likeness, that will be. And we won't allow anything to go wrong with this one. Mr. Catlin will make sure of that. He'll lock it in the strong-room, where no one will be able to get at it."

Soon afterwards, Rollison went back through the big main workshop, where so many people bustled about doing so many things—and where Daffodil was studying a face in the lamp-surrounded mirror. She was staring at it as Rollison passed, and most certainly saw his reflection, but she gave no sign of recognition.

"Good evening, sir," said Jolly. "How did things go today?"

"As planned and expected," Rollison replied. "I had another cast made this morning, and spent the afternoon wondering whether I'm the right man for the Prisoners' Aid Society. I disagreed with every suggestion put forward."

"People are so conventional, sir."

"Or else I'm obnoxiously awkward." Rollison went through into his study, and saw several letters on his desk. "I've promised to go over to Bill Ebbutt's club this evening, and they'll ply me with fish and chips, so take the evening off if you feel like it."

"Thank you, sir." Jolly spoke from the passage leading to the kitchen, and Rollison opened one letter, to find an invitation to speak at an obscure association's dinner and dance. He opened the second, which was a note of thanks for a donation to a Boys' Club, opened the third—and dropped it.

Face upwards on the desk lay a photograph of himself, full face.

One eye—the left eye—had been burned out, as if with a cigarette.

CHAPTER 3

DEEP MALICE

"THERE'S no doubt that it's been done with deep malice," Jolly said. Standing by Rollison and looking down on the photograph, his face was very grave. "Have you any idea at all who it might be?"

"Not yet," Rollison answered bleakly. "One or two things are obvious. The burner of holes has ready access to Madame Tussaud's."

"Ready access, sir?" Jolly's tone implied a question.

"Yes. Catlin took this photograph, and printed it himself in the dark-room behind the Exhibition. This must have been stolen from there." Rollison picked it up cautiously, by the edges. "See what you can find, will you?"

"At once," said Jolly.

He took the photograph gingerly; the hole in the eye seemed to get larger. He went off with it to his own quarters, where there was a box-room which he had converted into a forensic laboratory on a small scale. In there he could develop films, make elementary chemical tests with Bunsen burner and litmus paper, check for finger-prints, put specimens under a microscope, and generally play detective. This workshop, as he preferred to call it, had been built up slowly over many years; Rollison was fond of saying that Jolly had started it in order to show him, Rollison, the folly of pretending he could do what the Yard did, and gradually the more straightforward and customary aids to detection had grown on him. Now, he was fiercely proud of everything here.

He took a bottle of dusting powder off a shelf, dipped a small camel hair brush inside, and brushed over the edges of the photograph. Here and there a little of the powder adhered to the surface. Rollison, who had followed his man, looked over his shoulder.

Jolly said: "Rubbed clean, sir."

"All of them?"

"I think two show very slightly." Jolly selected two blurred spots, and brushed more powder off them. As he did so, Rollison took a visiting card out of his wallet. Without a word, he placed this on the bench by the side of the photograph. Jolly appeared to ignore it.

"There are two fragmentary prints, sir—a man's, I would say, arched pattern." He picked up a magnifying glass to examine his find. "Yes, sir—almost certainly tented arch." Without a word he handed the glass to Rollison, then dusted grey powder over the visiting card. Being white, it showed dirt very quickly. A print became visible and more clearly identifiable by the naked eye.

"Sir!"

"Yes?"

"They're identical."

"I thought they might be."

"Catlin's," breathed Jolly.

"The card he gave me when we first met," said Rollison. "Pity."

"*Pity*, sir?"

"There's nothing surprising about Catlin handling both," Rollison pointed out, and Jolly was crestfallen at over-looking the obvious. "Do you think the others were deliberately wiped off?"

"Yes, sir. If you look closer"—Jolly handed Rollison the magnifying glass—"you will see tiny bits of white fluff sticking to the smeared prints. I wonder it that means that the identifiable prints were left on deliberately."

"It could be," conceded Rollison. "Cunning or double

cunning, that's what we have to find out. Why should anyone at Madame Tussaud's want to scare the wits out of me?"

"Whoever it is, is wasting their time," Jolly said, sententiously.

"Don't you believe it," Rollison said. "A little more of this and I'll be afraid to go out without a bodyguard. Especially if anything happens to that second cast."

"Isn't that to be locked in a safe?"

"What do you mean?"

"It would need an expert safe-breaker to open such a place, surely."

"Or someone with a key," observed Rollison. "Do you know what I'm going to do?"

"Talk to Mr. Grice?" Jolly hazarded.

"No need to bring the Yard into this yet," said Rollison. "I'm going to be at the safe when the door's opened to-morrow morning. See if Catlin's in his office, will you?"

There was a telephone in the workshop, and Rollison picked up the photograph as Jolly dialled Madame Tussaud's, asked for Catlin, and waited. He seemed to hold on for a long time. Rollison, studying the prints, was in fact thinking of all the people he had met today; the face which most impressed itself on his mind was Daffodil's.

Jolly spoke. "If you will hold on, sir." He looked at Rollison. "Mr. Catlin's gone, but Mr. Bernard Tussaud is available."

"Thanks." Rollison took the telephone. "Mr. Tussaud? . . . Yes, Rollison here. I wonder if I could be present when . . . What time? . . . I'll be there just before nine, then. Oh, I wonder if the people I know could be present? . . . You, Mr. Catlin, Mr. Wilberforce and his assistant, Payne, isn't it? . . . Miss Eva and Miss Daffodil . . . I can't really say why, except that I would like to see how they react if anything should be wrong with the head . . . Oh, it has? . . . Good . . . I most certainly hope you're right . . . Yes . . . There will be two of us, myself and Mr. Jolly . . . J-O-L-L-Y . . . Thank you, Mr. Tussaud. Goodbye."

When he replaced the receiver, Rollison grinned at Jolly.

"They've already made a wax head, I'm told. Have you ever been to Madame Tussaud's?"

"On one occasion, sir, as a child."

"I didn't know it was so old," Rollison said.

"Oh, indeed," said Jolly. "In fact it was a travelling exhibition in 1802, and settled in Baker Street thirty-five years later. It moved to its present site in 1884, over eighty years ago, and I still have a few years before I'm eighty."

"I'm humbled. Where did you learn all this?"

"Mr. Catlin left a catalogue when he first came to see you," explained Jolly, simply.

"So you're an authority on Madame Tussaud's. I want you to be an authority on the people who'll be at the safe-opening ceremony in the morning, too," Rollison said. "That may be even more important."

Rollison could not really understand it, but next morning he felt on edge. It was ridiculous. Even if the wax cast was damaged, he wouldn't be. There were a dozen possible explanations of what had happened. He would have been less impressed but for the burned photograph. Now, he looked round at the people crowding the small office where an enormous safe stood in a corner, almost large enough to be a strong-room.

Catlin was nearest the door, talking earnestly to Miss Eva, whose dark head was close to his. She was a woman of medium build, brisk, pleasant, efficient. Wilberforce was glaring at them. Next to him was his melancholy assistant. Payne, who looked lost without his tools. Jolly was in a corner from which he could best see every member of the group when the safe was opened.

Eva said clearly: "No, I haven't seen or heard from her."

"Daffodil's not here," remarked Wilberforce in a loud whisper.

"What time does she usually get in?" asked Rollison.

"About half-past eight," answered Eva. "She invariably telephones if she's going to be more than a few minutes late."

Catlin said: "Bernard's late, too."

"Must have been delayed," Wilberforce remarked.

He broke off as footsteps sounded in the passage—a woman's. Everyone turned to look at the door, and Daffodil came in. She looked somewhat dishevelled, and seemed a little out of breath, but neither fact detracted from her attractiveness. She appeared to glance at every-one, and finally her gaze rested for a moment on Rollison, and her face became expressionless; almost mask-like.

Then Bernard Tussaud entered, a man in late middle-age, with a self-deprecating smile, a vaguely apologetic manner. His grey hair was brushed straight back from his forehead, and he blinked about him through the lenses of horn-rimmed spectacles.

"I'm sorry I'm late," he said generally. "Good morning, Mr. Rollison."

"Good morning."

"Would you like me to open the safe now?" Tussaud was not a man to waste time on preliminaries.

"Will you?"

Tussaud stepped forward with two keys in his hand. Catlin and Eva had to move for him to get by. Jolly, remarkably self-effacing, was watching them all. Rollison felt his blood run faster, with a rare but very real anxiety. There was a metallic sound as Tussaud unlocked one lock, then inserted a key in a second; it clicked back sharply.

"Shall I—" Catlin stepped forward, hand outstretched to pull the heavy door of the safe.

"I will do it," Tussaud said.

Rollison tried to get a glimpse of everyone, and one thing was certain; Daffodil's face was set most tightly, in what might well be apprehension. All of them except Bernard Tussaud were tense. He pulled the door open slowly, and almost at once Rollison had a shock.

He was there, inside the safe, staring out at himself.

He had only one eye.

Everyone could see that—everyone must have realised the truth almost on the instant. It was a long time before anyone moved, so flabbergasted were they all. At last, Bernard Tussaud pulled the door open wider. As he did so, Daffodil cried out: "No!" And she turned and pushed her way blindly out of the room.

"Daff!" called Catlin.

"I'll get her," Eva said, and ran after the younger woman.

Only Wilberforce and Tussaud seemed oblivious of Daffodil's reaction, and stared silently at the head of the Toff, at the one eye which stared so steadily, and the empty socket of the other. Everyone left in the room seemed stunned either by Daffodil's outburst, or by what they now saw.

Rollison went closer to the safe, placed a hand on either side of the head, and raised it. He brought it out and examined it, while the others stared, most of them still too shocked to speak. There was no other damage, as far as he could see; the bald head, the face and neck marked slightly from the imperfections in the cast, the ears and nose and lips and chin all unscathed.

Only that eye was mutilated.

Involuntarily, Rollison shivered.

"I know one thing," said Wilberforce. "Someone wants to make sure you don't ever get into the Exhibition, Mr. Rollison."

"I'm beginning to wonder whether it was such a good idea," said Bernard Tussaud. "What do you think now, Mr. Rollison?"

All of them turned to look at Rollison; even Jolly seemed to forget everyone else. Rollison remembered that involuntary shiver, forced a grin, and said:

"I've never wanted to be in the Chamber of Horrors so much. When will you make another head?"

Bernard Tussaud smiled in his dry, almost droll manner, and then took the mould out of the safe, peered inside it, and nodded with obvious satisfaction.

"This isn't damaged, so I'll cast you again this morning," he said. "I'm a stubborn man, too, when I have to be. Would you like to come up and see the head made?"

"I'd rather talk to Daffodil."

"Well, you can't," said Eva, coming in as Rollison spoke. "I don't think she's stopped running yet." Now it was Eva who held the audience. "She rushed downstairs. and when she couldn't get out the back way, ran right across the Grand Hall, flew down the stairs, and almost fell into the street. There were so many people about that I didn't see which way she went." Eva, facing Rollison, seemed to be steeling to add something else. "Mr. Rollison, what have you done to Daff? Why does she hate you so?"

"Hate," Wilberforce echoed.

"That's what I said, and that's what I mean." Eva's voice was shrill with the boldness of her effort.

"Eva," Rollison answered gently, "that's what I'm going to find out. Is your offer still open, Mr. Tussaud?"

"I am going to pour the wax myself," Bernard said. "The rest of you might as well do whatever you ought to be doing. Jim"—he spoke to Catlin—"the B.B.C. wants to talk to you, a Mr. Bateson at the Television Centre. Eva, we must have the head of the Sheik of Godol ready tomorrow. How are you getting on with the hair?"

"I'll finish it if I have to work all night," Eva promised.

Bernard led Rollison and Jolly to the main workshop. It was almost a surprise to find dozens of people working as if nothing remarkable had happened. Three big metal coppers full of beeswax were steaming, a huge kettle was on the gas ring and was coming to the boil. An unclad dummy of a tubby man, jauntily wearing a bowler hat, stood neglected near one wall; near him a suit hung on a hanger from a nail.

"I'm going to do everything myself," Bernard insisted. "Even take the beeswax out of the copper." He went to the middle copper and took off the lid. Jolly watched, fascinated. He dipped a wax-coated saucepan in and filled a big metal jug with molten wax. "Just like Brown Windsor soup, Mr. Jolly, isn't it?" He led the way to the bench on which stood the cast of Rollison's face, and as all the others watched he began to pour the hot wax in; it *was* like Brown Windsor.

A man nearby shouted:

"Watch it, Mr. Bernard!"

Bernard Tussaud stopped pouring.

"What's the matter?"

"The mould's cracked—look, wax is coming out."

Round the edges of the plaster mould the wax was oozing through cracks which were slowly getting wider. Suddenly, Bernard shouted: "Move back!" He pushed both Rollison and Jolly away and darted back himself as the mould split into several parts and the hot wax spilled out, splashing their clothes and shoes, and making a huge brown puddle on the stone floor.

Everyone in the workshop stood utterly still, as if all of them were made of wax which had suddenly solidified. Rollison moved first, bending down very slowly to pick up a piece of the wax. It appeared quite clean on the outside. He handled this carefully, aware that everyone was watching him; he could hear the breath whistling through Jolly's nostrils.

On the outside of the piece of plaster were marks, like small dents; hammer marks, obviously. He straightened up and looked about him. All sorts of tools were on a section of the long bench, including several hammers. The steel heads were all marked with plaster or wax— plaster, wax or powder seemed to cover every surface here.

"Just a question of which hammer," he remarked and turned to the bench.

Unexpectedly, Bernard Tussaud said: "That one." He took a hammer from the bench and held it out, head first, towards Rollison. One part of the head was thin and narrow, like the dents. Rollison took it, and placed that part against a dent; the fit was perfect.

"Everything happens here," Rollison said almost naïvely.

"I'm afraid so," said Tussaud.

"Who has access to this room?"

"Oh, dozens of people. Some are employed here, some are visitors, there are electricians and gas fitters, painters and decorators—*hundreds* of people, in fact," Bernard Tussaud declared.

"And how many of them have access to the safe?" asked Rollison.

Bernard Tussaud said quietly: "I do. Catlin does. My brother does."

"Just the three of you?"

"Yes."

"The safe was opened with a key."

"I know."

"Mr. Tussaud," Rollison said, "why don't you want my statue in your Exhibition?"

CHAPTER 4

HUNT FOR DAFFODIL

ALTHOUGH so many others were present, it seemed to Rollison as if Rollison and Tussaud were the only two people in the room. The older man's hand was smeared with the hard wax. Rollison still held the hammer and the piece of the mould. Behind his glasses, Tussaud's eyes seemed large and very earnest.

"You've guessed wrong," he said. "I would hardly need to adopt this kind of trickery to keep you out. I would simply refuse to have you. The board would support me, and there wouldn't be any argument. As a matter of fact—" he paused.

"Yes?" said Rollison gently.

"It was my idea to invite you."

"Not Catlin's?"

"No. Mine." Tussaud smiled faintly. "In a way you are unique, you know."

"What way?"

"You are on the borderline between being famous and being notorious."

Rollison was surprised into a laugh.

"I see what you mean. Who *is* doing this?"

"I really don't know," said Tussaud. "I can tell you one thing you may not have thought about."

"What thing?"

"This isn't necessarily a campaign against you."

"It looks very much like one."

"It could be against us."

"Tussaud's?"

"Yes."

"Why?"

"Don't we all have enemies?"

"Why should you have?"

Tussaud said: "Perhaps we ought to talk about that in private." He turned and led the way towards the door through which they had come, pausing just outside for Rollison and Jolly. "If we go to my office—"

"Give me a moment first," Rollison said, and turned to Jolly. "See what you can find out about Daffodil, Jolly. Especially try to find her."

"I'll be very glad to, sir," Jolly said.

"If you need assistance," Tussaud told him, "ask Mr. Catlin. He will tell you where Daffodil lives." He led the way again up a flight of stone steps in a building which was obviously very old, and into a tiny office, with a desk, two chairs and some bookshelves. He motioned to a chair, and spoke as Rollison sat down. "Mr. Rollison, we certainly do have enemies. Who they are we don't know, but from time to time we get letters threatening to burn the Exhibition down. From time to time we have figures damaged, obviously maliciously. These are isolated instances, to be sure, but such things have happened. This may be just another in a long line. I have been advised to go to the police, but the circumstances have never seemed sufficient to warrant that. Since you are already involved, will you investigate in whatever way you feel necessary?"

After a pause, Rollison asked: "Suppose this is simply a vendetta against me?"

"Whether it is or not you will have to check thoroughly

to find out the instigator. In so doing, you might well solve our problem, too. I hope you won't say no, Mr. Rollison."

"I've seldom been more eager to say yes, but on one condition."

"Please name it."

"That I can have the run of the Exhibition, the offices and the workshops, and—"

"That goes without saying."

"And that anyone I nominate may have the same facilities."

"Naturally."

"I may want you to take several of them on your payroll."

"It is never very easy to get staff," said Bernard Tussaud. He gave his rather droll smile, then added: "May I make a practical suggestion?"

"Please."

"Do everything through me, please. Only use Catlin whenever you must, and use none of the other staff as intermediaries. If you want a man or a dozen men to become temporary members of the staff, approach Catlin or me."

"Do you actually know it's an inside job?" asked Rollison. "Or do you just suspect it?"

"It looks very nearly certain, doesn't it?" Tussaud said quietly.

After another, longer pause, Rollison looked away from Bernard Tussaud's eyes, glancing upwards at an old oil painting on the wall over the desk. It was large for the room; too large in fact. It was a faded portrait of an elderly woman, wearing steel-rimmed spectacles and a bonnet.

"Is that the original Madame Tussaud?" he asked.

"Yes. My great-great-grandmother."

"One other condition, Mr. Tussaud."

"What is it?"

"That nothing stops you from putting my likeness on show."

"You can be quite sure that nothing will," asserted Bernard. "But at the present rate of progress it may take rather a long time."

Rollison chuckled.

"How will you begin your investigations?" asked Tussaud.

"With Daffodil, when we've found her. What can you tell me about her?"

"Very little, I fear—except of her disruptive effect on younger male members of the staff. She has a great deal of a potent kind of sex appeal. She joined us straight from the Central London Art School, where she gained a diploma in design."

"Design," echoed Rollison. "Why switch to make-up, I wonder?"

"There is one thing you probably don't realise," observed Bernard Tussaud. "Clay and wax modelling, in fact any kind of modelling, has a great appeal to some people. I believe that Daffodil set her mind on getting a job here, and virtually besieged the place. She really wanted to make the clay heads, but she isn't qualified, nor even very adept. Eva needed assistance in the make-up and colouring section, and Daffodil jumped at the chance. She's been very good. The place is in her blood, so to speak."

"Has she any relatives here?"

"Oh, I don't mean literally in her blood," said Bernard. "None of your relations is in the police force, I imagine."

Rollison chuckled again.

"Not yet," he said. "Tell Catlin I'll probably be in later, won't you?"

"Of course," promised Bernard. "Can you find your way out?"

"Easily," Rollison said.

In fact, he took a wrong passage, and found himself in an unfamiliar hall, with a surging crowd of sightseers moving slowly from tableau to tableau. There was a general cackle of conversation as well as the steady shuffling of feet. A few elderly commissionaires stood about, keeping an eye on the movement of the crowd. No one appeared to take any special notice of Rollison. He found the main staircase and went down to the hall. On the right was the Hall of Dioramas, where just as many people walked about the machines. Throngs were coming in at the main door, and Rollison went out that way.

It was very hot in the street, a reminder of the air-conditioning in the Exhibition.

Still no one appeared to take any notice of him.

He got into a taxi, turned to make sure he wasn't followed, then suddenly asked himself why he was so much on edge. He made himself turn round and stare straight in front of him, until he got out of the taxi.

He was up the stone steps of the house in Gresham Terrace, to his flat right at the top. There was no sound anywhere. He listened at the door for a minute, before opening it with his key. He kept the door ajar, and called:

"Jolly!"

There was no answer.

Why should he expect one? He had sent Jolly to look for Daffodil.

He went into the living-room, which was empty—of course it was. The damaged photograph was still on the desk. As he stared at it, he remembered putting it near a corner, and now it was close to the middle of the front, where he might have put it had he been sitting there.

He had not sat at that desk since receiving the photograph.

He opened the middle drawer, and saw some papers out of position; where his desk was concerned he was always meticulously tidy. He opened other drawers, and had no doubt at all that the desk had been searched.

He stood up, slowly. It was possible that whoever had searched the desk was still in the flat. He moved towards the door leading to the bedrooms, bathroom and the domestic quarters, but heard no sound. He put his head round every door, and found each room empty until only the kitchen was left. He pushed that door open, slowly.

Jolly was at the sink, back to the door, a green baize apron tied round his waist, shirt sleeves startlingly white against a black waistcoat, and a puckering billow of shirt showing between the waistcoat and the waistband of the grey trousers.

"Good lord!" exclaimed Rollison. "Didn't you hear me?"

Jolly showed no sign that he had heard even that. Alarm ran through Rollison, and he stepped forward quickly.

"Jolly! Are you all right?"

His man neither moved nor spoke. Rollison reached him, and gripped his arm.

"Jolly—"

His voice trailed off, for Jolly swayed, as if he had no muscular control, as if he were—dead.

Rollison steadied him and then peered at his face.

It was not Jolly. It was a dummy with a wax face which was just the shape of an egg, a blank, featureless face with a hole where the left eye ought to be.

"Now why?" the Toff asked himself.

"And who?" he wanted to know.

"And when—"

The timing was at least easy to establish. He and Jolly had left here at half-past eight. It was a firm house-rule that no other servant should be here when both Rollison and Jolly were out, and Jolly had a flexible arrangement with a domestic agency. No one else had a key, either back or front. Rollison went through the kitchen to the back door, and saw at once that this break-in had been done by an expert. The double-mortice lock had been forced.

"Very professional," murmured Rollison. He opened the back door and looked down into a small, concrete-paved courtyard, empty, bare and bleak. A service road led into it from the left-hand side, and each building surrounding the square had an iron fire-escape-cum-service staircase which served all the flats.

Rollison saw nothing on the platform immediately outside. Neighbours and their servants might be able to give some information, but it would hardly be surprising if no one had seen the dummy delivered. Large parcels and crates were not uncommon, for Rollison read many books, and Jolly had a system by which furniture and pictures were taken away for repair, cleaning and renovation at regular intervals.

Rollison went back into the kitchen, studied the effigy, and said *sotto voce:*

"It shouldn't have fooled me." Then: "Why go to the trouble of dressing him up—why try to hoax me?" After a moment he added explosively: "Some hoax!"

As the word faded away, the telephone bell rang.

There was an instrument on a shelf by the kitchen window.

"Rollison," announced Rollison.

"I'm glad you're back, sir," said Jolly, promptly.

"Have you found the lady?" asked Rollison.

"No, but some rather unexpected facts have emerged, sir."

"Such as?"

"Daffodil moved from her only known address two days ago."

"*Only* known?" exclaimed Rollison.

"No one at the address knows where she went," Jolly

reported. "It is a flat shared by five young ladies—all rather arty young ladies, sir."

"And Daffodil just walked out on them?"

"As I understand it she simply didn't come back after leaving for work on the Monday of this week. May I suggest you come here, sir? Two of the co-tenants are in, but not exactly being co-operative. I think they might be with you."

"I'll come," Rollison said. "What's the address?"

"Flat 8, 17 Conning Square, Knightsbridge," answered Jolly. "An aunt of Daffodil lives at Putney. Shall I go and interview her?"

"Later," Rollison said. "Come back here, and don't worry too much about the piece of statuary in the kitchen."

Where another man would have echoed 'Statuary' or burst out with questions, Jolly gave an almost imperceptible pause, before saying: "Very good, sir."

"Where are you speaking from?" asked Rollison.

"A telephone in the apartment. The two young ladies are up in the attic studio, out of earshot. I shall leave the apartment door ajar for you."

"Won't they answer a call?"

"I think if you wait until you see the situation for yourself you will understand more readily," Jolly said.

Number 17 Conning Square was one of the many small squares in that residential area between Brompton Road and the Albert Hall. Rollison's taxi passed the end of an attractive mews, where many stables had been converted to maisonettes and no one had spared fresh paint, and entered the square of tall, almost forbidding grey houses, with pillared porticos looking too large for the front doors, a few freshly painted but most of them drab. Outside three were house agents' reading: TO LET—UNFURNISHED FLAT, or FOR SALE—SUITABLE FOR CONVERSION.

There was no board outside Number 17.

Rollison gave his driver a pound, and said: "Wait, will you?"

"Certainly, gov'nor."

The front door was closed, but opened when Rollison pushed it. Just inside the porch was a list of tenants' names opposite flat numbers. The top flat, 8, had such a list, and he studied it and began to smile. There was a brightly drawn *motif* opposite each name, all done with skill and also with a lively sense of humour, or at least of fun. The list read:

Norah—opposite an ark in black
Isobel—opposite a bell in blue
Daff—opposite a daffodil in yellow
Mandy—opposite a man's face in brown
Liz—opposite a Queen's crown in silver

Rollison repeated the names—Norah, Isobel, Daff, Mandy and Liz—as he went towards the stairs. The inside of the house was brighter than the outside. All the flats were self-contained, two at each landing with brightly painted doors. The top flight of stairs was narrower than the others, and this led to the olden-day servants' quarters. At the top there was a tiny landing and only one door. The door was painted in horizontal lines, black, blue, yellow, brown and silver.

As Jolly had promised, the door was ajar.

Rollison pushed it wider, and stepped into a big room of many colours, so many colours that the first impression was overpowering. In fact, it was not. It was not a pattern yet there was some kind of order or design: it was like an abstract painting, in which couches and chairs, cushions and rugs, tables and bookcases, even the radio and pale blue telephone had a part in the design.

One wall, opposite the two large windows, was an abstract mural on a huge scale. The other walls and the ceiling were plain off-white.

Rollison moved towards a door at the far end. It led to a huge barn of a bathroom with a gurgling cistern, to a kitchen and to two bedrooms, one with three divans, one with two. These were strictly utilitarian, with cheap, old-fashioned furniture, an absolute minimum of comfort.

Beyond the passage was a wooden ladder, like one leading up into a hayloft. It was daubed with paint of many colours. Rollison did not call or go up immediately, but went into the bedrooms. There were so many intimate little feminine things about that he felt a real sense of intrusion. A bra tossed over the back of a wooden chair, a blue hair-net draped over a pot of cream, a deodorant next to a tin of talcum powder, some hairpins and hairgrips, stocking on the floor, a pair of panties half inside and half out of a chest of drawers.

Which of these beds was Daffodil's?

It was impossible to guess, and none of the furniture was marked with the names or symbols. He could waste a lot of time searching here.

Rollison turned back to the ladder and went slowly and cautiously upwards. He did not hear a sound, but as his head rose above floor level he saw in front of him two pairs of legs, one pair sturdy and with very full calves, one pair thin but shapely. He took another step up the ladder, and now he could see that the two girls, their backs towards him, were working on the same piece of canvas. Both seemed so intent that they were oblivious of him.

Yet in one way they were very much aware of him.

One was just finishing a huge symbol of the Toff, a drawing which he had used for years. It was blue on white, stark and startling:

The other had made a savage, almost cruel caricature of him, yellow on black with some streaks of red, the clear bright red of blood.

CHAPTER 5

IS AND LIZ

As he watched, Rollison became more sure that the girls knew he was there, and that part of their intentness was an effort to fool him. The girl on the right, doing the Toff symbol, was tall and slender, dressed in short pants, boyish—at least from behind. The other was dumpy, yet shapely. She wore tennis shorts which fell over her hips and bottom with a fine sweep; it was a reasonable guess that nothing about her was boyish. Her short hair was a lovely chestnut colour, and the thin girl's was jet black— and swept up almost in Edwardian style.

They kept on working.

Rollison hoisted himself up into the studio, making a noise which they could not fail to hear, yet they showed no sign that they had. He glanced round. There were four easels in different position, all under a huge north light in the roof. On two easels were half-finished canvases, but the others were empty. Near this, against the wall, were several sheets of hardboard, often used by young artists because it was cheaper than canvas. Everywhere about the studio stood finished and partly-finished paintings of all shapes, sizes, colours, conditions and manner, from the most obscure abstract to quite straightforward impressionist portraits. In one corner was a bench with a half-finished male nude statue on it. On a shelf above this were some miniature heads, and as Rollison drew nearer he recognized two of them as Daffodil. There were five pairs, one of each wax, the other plaster. The bench looked rather like the plaster bench at Madame Tussaud's.

Rollison walked to the empty easel, without saying a word. He picked up a piece of hardboard and placed it in position, then selected a brush from a dozen stuck in an old jampot, and picked up a small palette, thick and rich with oil paint.

He filled his brush with green, and stood back to study the empty canvas. The girls, behind him, were now staring, although they still held their brushes.

With bold strokes, Rollison printed: *"And then there were 4. Where's Daff?"*

One of the girls gave a little giggle of a laugh. The other laughed more loudly.

"Very funny," this one said.

"It depends what you're thinking about," said Rollison. "Surely you can divine that."

The speaker was the tall, slim girl: There was nothing boyish about her from the front view. The short girl seemed all torso, and no neck at all. Each of them was the original of two of the small heads on the shelf.

"We were thinking about you," the tall girl went on. "As your man was here we expected you, and thought you would like your portrait painted."

"All nice, clean fun," murmured Rollison. "Where's Daff?"

"Don't you know?"

"Not yet."

"Perhaps she doesn't want to be found," suggested the short girl. "What do you think, Liz?"

"I don't know, Is," replied the tall girl.

So one was Liz and the other was Is, obviously short for Isobel. Both were half-laughing, but in Liz's dark blue eyes there seemed to lurk more seriousness than in Is's. Is had a broad, round face and a button of a nose, the nostrils showing black; heavy eyebrows and very dark lashes.

She had a big mouth, which was not very shapely. Liz had a pleasant face, the nose and mouth just a little out of true, giving her a kind of lopsided look.

"Liz," said Rollison. "Give Daffodil a message for me, will you?"

"I might, and I might not. It depends whether I know where she is."

"What message?" asked Is.

"That if she hasn't telephoned me by six o'clock this evening to make an appointment, I shall notify the police that she is missing."

Is exclaimed: "You can't do that!"

"Why not? Isn't she missing?"

"Oh, *very clever,*" Liz said, half-angry, half-sarcastic. "She'll never telephone you."

"Then by six-fifteen the Yard will have posted her as missing and by tomorrow the newspapers will be asking people if they have seen her."

"They'd never listen to you," Liz said.

"Newspapers always listen."

"I mean the police wouldn't."

"They would when I told them she was wanted in connection with a series of crimes."

"What on earth are you saying?" cried Is.

Rollison smiled sweetly at Liz.

"You know what I'm saying, don't you?" He turned away, quite leisurely but with an air of finality, as if that was the last word.

"Liz, say something to him!" Is burst out. "Stop him!"

"And I'd always heard that the man known as the Toff had a wonderful sense of humor," Liz mocked. "He's as solemn as an owl."

"On this occasion, he's simply serious," said Rollison over his shoulder.

He was now nearly at a disadvantage, for he could not walk forward down the ladder, an expanding one; it was too steep; he would have to turn to face the girl, and so spoil the effect of his little plan. At least he was virtually sure that they knew where Daffodil was.

As he reached the top of the ladder, Liz spoke in a flat voice.

"Toff."

He turned his head.

"Yes?"

"If Daffodil telephones, I'll give her your message."

"I hope she calls before six o'clock this evening," Rollison said.

"A lot of things can happen between now and six o'clock," reported Liz.

"Why are you so anxious to talk to her?" demanded Isobel.

Rollison took the opportunity to turn his back onto the hatch and the ladder. Liz looked coldly supercilious, the dumpy girl angry but anxious.

"I want to know what she hates, whom she hates, and why."

"*Daff* doesn't hate anybody!"

"Doesn't she?" asked Rollison, and stepped back to the top rung.

It wasn't there.

As he lowered his foot, sure of himself because he had the ladder clearly in his mind's eye, he felt the moment of unbalance, the awful second when the inevitability of disaster is apparent. He had put so much weight down that he could not steady himself. In a kaleidoscopic preview of what would happen he saw himself falling backwards, banging his head on the far side of the hatch, dropping down half-conscious if not unconscious, perhaps breaking a leg or an arm—or his neck.

He did the only possible thing which might help, springing backwards and lifting both legs in a kind of backward running jump. As he went, he saw the extending ladder leaning against the wall, and he grabbed at it to break his fall. He clutched, lost his grip, and clutched again. This time he only touched the ladder, but already he had broken his fall, and he landed and rolled over with a heavy jolt, but nothing worse. He lay on the floor for a moment, looking upwards. Two faces, Liz's oval and clear, Isobel's round and sallow against her chestnut hair, were framed by the hatch which led into the studio.

Very slowly, Rollison began to get up.

He was furiously angry, but kept his wits about him enough to know that he must not show it. He was badly shaken and slightly shocked. He reached his feet, and dusted himself down, without looking up again at the two girls. The ladder had simply been pushed two yards away —anyone could have done it.

He turned away, still without looking up. Passing the bedroom doors, he had a mental picture of Daffodil, slender and certainly not powerful.

By the time he reached the street, he was able almost to laugh at himself, and he was at the nearer corner when an obvious thing occurred to him so unexpectedly that it brought a sharp sense of shock.

The girls had made a fool of him, in two ways—they had hoaxed him very well indeed. But was it malicious, like the damage to the wax face and to the cast?

He beckoned to the waiting taxi-driver to follow him, and walked towards Brompton Road at a leisurely pace, partly to allow anyone who followed a good chance to catch up with him, partly to make sure he had good time to recover. As far as he could tell, only the taxi followed, slowly. The traffic in the main street was fast, furious and thick, a motor-age cacophony assailed his ears. He crossed the road at a zebra crossing, then turned and stood watching the turning which led to Conning Square. Two elderly women came along it, one youth far too small and slight to have moved the ladder, and a policeman.

The policeman puzzled Rollison. Most men who had been in the Force for years walked with a positive although indefinable deliberation, as if they knew exactly where they were going and the best way to get there. They took long strides, and had a habit of looking about them, as if they had all the time in the world, and meant to miss nothing.

This man looked straight ahead. He walked hurriedly, without the habitual deliberation. He was rather short and powerfully built, and his uniform seemed too big for him. He reached the corner of the street opposite Rollison, looked quickly up and down, and then broke into a run for a bus which was just moving from a stop. Rollison's own taxi was just alongside, and the driver had the door open. Rollison jumped in as it was moving, slammed the door, and placed his mouth close to the sliding panel between him and the driver.

"Follow that Number 14 bus."

"It's your neck, guv. How far?"

"Until a policeman gets off."

"A copper?" The driver was putting the nose of the taxi towards a narrow gap in the traffic.

"Yes."

"Got it the wrong way round, haven't you? He ought to be following you. I—oh. Ta!"

Rollison slipped another pound note over the man's shoulder, then sat back, crossed his ankles and relaxed.

The burst of activity had done him good, and would do him much more if the chase of the policeman proved worthwhile. Now and again he saw the bus; he could see the platform and would know the moment the policeman appeared. He felt quite himself again, although more rueful than ever. The girls had certainly made a fool of him.

Was it just for kicks?

He kept seeing Liz in his mind's eye; not dumpy Isobel, but tall, almost arrogant, certainly aloof Liz. Every now and again a girl made a real impression on him; he had a feeling that Liz had done exactly that.

The driver called: "Copper!"

The stocky policeman was stepping onto the platform of the bus as they approached the nearest stop to Piccadilly Circus.

"I'm going to follow him on foot," Rollison said. "Try to keep contact, will you?" He opened the door as the cab pulled in at the kerb, and jumped out. The policeman was already walking towards the Circus, still quite brisk; Rollison had the impression that he was much more at ease now. He walked round Swan & Edgars, and waited at the bus stop in Regent Street. The taxi drew alongside Rollison and the driver beckoned. Rollison got in again and as he sat back, a bus passed, only to pull up alongside the bus stop. The policeman got on, and went upstairs.

The driver twisted round to look at Rollison.

"Same drill?" he asked.

"Yes. What's the number of the bus?"

"59A," he answered. "Baker Street, Park Road, St. John's Wood."

Although he gave the route as well as if he had been a bus conductor, Rollison hardly heard him beyond "St. John's Wood." This bus crossed Marylebone Road, very close to Madame Tussaud's.

Would the policeman get off there?

Rollison felt so certain that he allowed himself to look about him and even to enjoy the morning sunshine. Only when they crossed the Marylebone Road towards St. John's Wood did he pay attention to the bus ahead. He almost tapped at the window, but the driver had proved himself to be alert enough.

The bus stopped at Baker Street Station, but the policeman did not get off. It stopped several times on the way to Lord's Cricket Ground, and two or more passengers alighted at each stop, but not the policeman. At the stop past Lord's, the driver looked round.

"Having a nice long ride, sir?"

Rollison said: "Get in front of the bus, will you? I want to have a look on the top deck." With casual expertise the driver passed the bus and put on a spurt, pulling up at a request stop, several hundred yards in front of the Number 59A.

Rollison had a choky feeling as he got off, waited for the bus, got on, glanced past the Jamaican conductor and made sure the policeman was not inside, then clambered up on top. He stood stock still at the head of the stairs, oblivious of the conductor, whose soft voice pleaded:

"Move along the bus, sir, please."

Rollison gulped.

"Sorry."

He moved to one side, staring at seven women, three children and five men—all in ordinary clothes, none of them wearing even a policeman's helmet.

The soft voice was very insistent.

"Move along, sir, please."

Rollison said: "Yes." He put a sixpence into the man's hand, and moved a few seats along, but he knew that he was wasting his time up here. The 'policeman' must have changed his clothes, or else—

"Excuse me," the conductor was saying to a passenger in the back seat, "is this yours, sir?"

The man said: "No."

"May I have it, please?" The conductor stretched past the passenger and picked up a heavy blue tunic and a pair of trousers. Beneath these was a policeman's helmet. The explanation was very simple; the 'policeman' had got a back seat, peeled off his clothes, and left the bus.

CHAPTER 6

VOLUNTEERS

"It beats me," the taxi-driver said as Rollison got out of the taxi in the Mile End Road, near a big new block of flats. "I didn't see him—I swear I didn't."

"Nor did I," said Rollison sadly.

The man put his hand to his pocket, and his blue eyes had an earnest expression.

"How about taking a quid back?"

The offer was so spontaneous that Rollison had to laugh.

"You earned it," he said.

"Easy money," declared the driver. "See you around, I hope."

He moved off into a stream of heavy truck traffic, snarling, pulsating towards the docks and the east coast. Rollison moved towards a street which reflected the centuries. It did not seem quite right to come here to London's East End and find that at one end of the street were fine apartment buildings, while at the far end there were two rows of small, grey terraced homes, the front doors opening straight onto the pavement, doors so close together that each 'house' was little more than a hut.

In fact, some were hovels and some were palaces; and Rollison knew a dozen of each.

He stood at the next corner, between the old and the new. Traffic noises had receded, the nearer sounds were of youngsters shouting, a baby crying, two women talking, a radio on too loud. After the aloofness and the tall, quiet houses of Mayfair, this made a strange contrast. And after Mayfair, this part of the East End of London was closest to Rollison's heart. He knew the place and the people. He knew how much better the new flats were to live in, and yet he felt a kind of resentment based on nostalgia for the old places which first the bombs 'and then the bulldozers had crunched, crumbled, and turned into dust.

He crossed the street, diagonally. From this point looking south towards the Thames, the skyline was unchanged. Not even a great square warehouse was new. Every brick had the grime of more than half a century, every distant crane made a familiar etching against the sky. The masts of some ships and the funnels of others showed against the broken skyline.

Nearer at hand were the terraced houses, not far beyond were the narrow alleys between high warehouse walls, and nearer at hand was the familiar red brick of the Blue Dog, a pub of great renown. Outside it swung a new inn sign, which Rollison had not seen before; it reminded him that it was at least six months since he had been down here. The dog was a mongrel, sky blue in colour, a lively little terrier type, very well painted.

Painted!

Rollison's thoughts flashed to the attic studio where he had nearly broken his neck.

Two or three men went into the pub. Rollison followed, still a little shaken both by the fall and the failure to follow the phoney policeman. The saloon bar was hot, stuffy, beery, and familiar. Only six people were here, but the rush would come later, it was not yet one o'clock. A young man whom he did not know was drawing beer from behind the bar for the men who had just come in. The wooden floorboards were covered with sawdust, soft and loose underfoot. A few photographs dotted the walls, all of pugilists in fighting pose, most of them yellow with age.

On the wall behind the bar was a photograph of Rollison himself.

The strange young man looked up.

"What's for you, sir?"

Rollison said: "Half of 4 XXXX."

"Right." The youth pulled the handle and beer foamed out precisely to the top of the glass. "One and a penny, sir."

Rollison stared.

"One and a penny, sir, if you please."

"Ah," said Rollison. "Yes, of course." He put his hand to his pocket, feeling rather as if he were in a strange new world, for it was many years since he had paid for a drink in the Blue Dog. He placed a two shilling piece on the bar, and as he did so three things happened.

A door at the side of the bar opened and a big man appeared.

The youth's hand stretched out for the two shilling piece.

A man in the corner cried: "It's Mr. Ar!"

The big man, Ebbutt—he was even fatter than Rollison remembered—stopped in his tracks, and echoed:

"Mr. *Ar*!"

The barman picked up the two shilling piece.

"What the hell are you doing?" roared the big man. He almost leaped forward, snatched the coin up, and thrust it back at Rollison. "Well, what a sight for sore eyes. Who'd a thought it? I told Lil it was a lucky day, only this morning. Mr. Ar, how *are* yer?"

He held out his great hand, still calloused from the ring fights of his youth. He was not handsome, for he had a big broad face, pinky in colour, blue veined at the cheeks and the nose, with a spade of a chin and a little bud of a mouth. But there was a glow in his deepset eyes and pleasure in his wheezing voice. He wrung Rollison's hand as if he would twist it off.

"Well, how *are* yer? How's Jolly? What's been keeping you away? Haven't been ill, have yer? How're tricks? Seen old Gricey lately? Blimey, you're sight for sore eyes, you are. Don't take no notice of Archie here, only been working for a coupla months, don't know the house rules yet. Archie, this is Mr. Rollison. *The* Mr. Rollison. Wake up, son, don't look so daft. The *Toff*! Don't you never so much as look as if you would take money from him in future."

"The Toff," breathed Archie, who was small as well as youthful, pale as well as ignorant; and certainly overawed.

"Remember me?" It was the man who had spoken from the corner, approaching Rollison eagerly, hand outstretched. "Tiny Higgins."

"I haven't lost my memory yet, Tiny." Rollison shook hands, and looked back at Bill Ebbutt. "Well, Bill. You look fine."

"Couldn't be better, Mr. Ar—at least I didn't think I could, until I saw you. Can you have a bite to eat with Lil and me?"

"I'd love to."

"Archie, go and tell the missus I'll be bringing a guest for lunch. Don't tell who it is, mind. I want to see her face when she sets eyes on Mr. Ar. Cor strewth . . ." and on and on he went.

Twenty minutes, nine old friends and three 4 XXXX half pints later, Rollison was led to the back of the bar, out into the yard, and up the stairs to the living quarters of the Blue Dog. Here everything was the same, even to the appetising aroma coming from the first-floor kitchen. The yard itself was scrupulously clean; a few crates of empties and some barrels on trestles stood in neat array, with some coils of rope. Over one wall the top of a wooden building showed—a gymnasium owned and operated by Ebbutt, who trained both amateurs and professionals in what he insisted on calling the fistic art.

"Don't say a word," he whispered. "Ears like a fox, Lil has." He put a fat forefinger to his lips as he led the way up a flight of stairs, their oaken banisters and rail shiny with much polishing, everything having an unmistakable sparkle.

"Smells good," Ebbutt went on in a clear voice. "Steak and kidney pie, I'd say. Hey! Lil! Got 'a guest for dinner!"

He led the way past a spacious looking living-room into a small dining-room where a table was laid for three, damask cloth white and shimmering, cutlery gleaming. As they stepped through, Lil Ebbutt came briskly out of the kitchen, a little woman with rather sharp features, bright blue eyes, hair still almost black in spite of her sixty years.

"You might have told—" she began; and then she saw Rollison.

She raised her hands to her slender bosom, taken right aback. She drew in a short, sharp breath, and then advanced towards Rollison, with both hands outstretched. She was delighted.

"Well, well, Mr. Rollison! I'd no idea. My, you look well." She gripped his hands and he drew her towards him and kissed her firmly on the cheeks. "Bill said you'd deserted us, but I knew better." As she scanned his face, there was something maternal in her attitude and her expression. "My, it's good to see you!"

"Lil," said Rollison. "Every time I see you you really do look younger."

"It's the way I treat her," Ebbutt put in smugly.

"Don't listen to him," Lil said. "He's the only worry I've got." She took her hands away. "I hope you're hungry."

"As a hunter," Rollison assured her.

"Look after him for a minute, while I dish up," Lil ordered her husband, and whisked herself off to the kitchen.

"Don't change much, does she?" remarked Ebbutt proudly. "Do you know what? She's being promoted. After next month she'll be a major."

"Better be careful she doesn't go too high in the Army," Rollison warned.

"No telling how high she'll go. Still nags at me to give up the pub and lead a good sin-free life, bless her heart."

Rollison reflected on these remarkable people, the ex-prize fighter publican, and the little, fiery woman whose life was divided in some improbable way between the Salvation Army and her man. She bustled in with a huge steak pie, the crust flaky and golden brown.

"Wonderful meal," Rollison said, twenty-five minutes later. "No more, Lil. Absolutely no more."

"Getting old, that's your trouble." Lil had eaten heartily herself, and looked comfortably replete. Without batting an eyelid, she went on: "I suppose you've come to ask Bill to help in this Madame Tussaud's trouble."

"This *what?*" gasped Ebbutt.

"Didn't think he'd come just for old times' sake, did you?"

Lil looked at Rollison with a gleam in her eyes. She was delighted, not because she had so astonished her husband but because Rollison was staring at her. She might almost have guessed that she had shaken him to the core.

"Madame Tussaud's," Ebbutt said, wheezing. "What's all this?"

"How did you know, Lil?" asked Rollison. "Did Jolly—?"

"Jolly nothing," interrupted Lil briskly. "It was on the radio."

Rollison was even more surprised.

"When?"

"Half-past twelve, and again at half-past one."

"What did it say?" demanded Ebbutt.

"It said that a wax head of Mr. Rollison's had been damaged, the first time there's been any trouble at Madame Tussaud's since someone pinched the statue of Lord Snowdon," Lil answered. "Didn't you know it was going to be on the news?"

"I did not," Rollison said, feelingly.

It was in the evening newspapers too, a front-page story in each, with a photograph that almost did Rollison justice, and the general outline of what had happened but with little detail. Rollison read both newspapers in his living-room-cum-study, at about five o'clock. He had been back for half-an-hour, time in which Bill Ebbutt had promised to supply as many of his 'boys' as needed for temporary duty at Madame Tussaud's. Each 'boy' was a tough boxer or ex-boxer, who knew Rollison well and who felt towards him much as Ebbutt did.

"I'm very relieved, sir," Jolly had said.

He stared at the two front pages, his face touched with alarm, almost with concern.

"Get Catlin on the telephone," Rollison said.

"Very good." Jolly went to the desk, and dialled while

Rollison put the newspapers down, went to the window and looked down into Gresham Terrace. The usual few pedestrians and lines of parked cars were there.

"Mr. Catlin, sir."

Rollison moved to the telephone.

"I know what you've called about—but I'm as baffled as you," Catlin said almost before Rollison had a chance to speak. "I didn't release the story, no one at Madame Tussaud's did—not officially, anyhow."

"But it leaked," said Rollison. "Have the press been to see you?"

"They've streamed in by the dozen."

"Have you given them details?"

"Only the bare bones of the story. Haven't you seen any newspapermen?" asked Catlin.

"Not yet." Rollison realised that was both true and surprising.

"They'll soon be worrying you."

"Have you heard from Daffodil?" asked Rollison.

"Not a word."

"Has anything else happened?"

"Nothing about you," answered Catlin. "Did you arrange for those tough pals of yours to come?"

"They'll all apply for a job tomorrow morning," Rollison said. "And they'll all draw the top hat symbol, to show that they're from me."

"Then we'll give them jobs where they can watch everywhere that matters," promised Catlin. "They'll be absolutely reliable, won't they?"

"Absolutely," Rollison assured him. He replaced the receiver, looked into Jolly's anxious face, and asked without a change of tone: "What did you say to the press, Jolly?"

"That you wouldn't be home until late tonight, sir."

"And they believed you," marvelled Rollison. "They're getting too gullible."

"You didn't want them, did you?"

"Not yet," said Rollison. "Certainly not until we know whether Daffodil is coming. Jolly."

"Sir?"

"Have you any idea at all what this is all about?"

"Nothing positive," Jolly answered. "In fact nothing that isn't so obvious it hardly seems reasonable to consider it."

"The Franken sons and daughters?"

"Yes."

"How hard do they hate?"

Jolly said in a quiet voice which seemed to contain a note of alarm:

"Very much indeed."

"But it's six months ago."

"Do you really think that would make any difference?" asked Jolly. "You were undoubtedly responsible—directly responsible—for the conviction and execution of the husband and wife." When Rollison didn't answer, Jolly went on: "And they were a very devoted family."

"Like parents, like children, you mean."

"In a manner of speaking, yes."

Rollison moved towards the Trophy Wall, and contemplated it almost gloomily. At one side, beneath a test tube containing arsenic and above a flick knife which had been used in a gang-murder, was the latest exhibit in this remarkable collection. The exhibit was very simple, and did not look in any way lethal. It was in fact a small piece of a black shoe-lace, with the metal end still attached. This trifle had begun the long investigation into the death of a wealthy South African, Ben Franken, who had been murdered in a London hotel. His only relatives, a family who lived in Chelsea, near the river, had been his heirs—to nearly half-a-million pounds, mostly in land and diamonds. He was one of the few men who had made a lucky strike in territory not controlled by the major diamond companies, and he had come to England to sell large quantities of stones, bringing them with him.

He had been robbed and murdered.

At first, the crime had been put down as a burglary, discovered by Ben, who had put up a fight. According to the Frankens, they had talked to the old man on the telephone, but never seen him. The curious kind of chance which so often led murderers to the gallows, had led Rollison to discover the piece of shoe-lace, made in Johannesburg, South Africa, in the Franken family's house in Clapham.

The shoe-lace was proved to be Ben's. From that point, the police established that he had visited his relatives and from there on it had been a long, slow, laborious compiling of circumstantial evidence, leading finally to proof that the senior Frankens had visited their relative on the night of his death. In a frantic attempt to save themselves, they had attacked and killed a policeman.

So, they had been hanged.

They had left three children, a girl Ethel and two boys, Jack and Arthur, in their early twenties.

"Jolly," Rollison said.

"Yes, sir."

"Norah, Isobel, Daffodil, Mandy and Elizabeth."

"I have their surnames from the caretaker at the house where they have their flat." Jolly took a typewritten list from a folder on Rollison's desk.

"Thanks." Rollison began to read aloud. "Norah Thomas, Isobel Allington, Daffodil Lee, Mandy Fitzherbert, Elizabeth Bonham. Have you started any further check?"

"Not yet, sir."

"We want to know their relatives and friends. They're about the right age for the Franken boys, for instance. They could have had substantial expectations, but now the money's held in Chancery—isn't it?"

"The South African equivalent, I understand," Jolly agreed.

"So we need any tenuous line which leads from one of them, preferably Daffodil Lee, to the Frankens."

"May I make a suggestion?" asked Jolly.

"Yes."

"The simple way to find out the answers would be to consult Superintendent Grice. In the circumstances he would certainly assist us, and now that the news has reached the newspapers it will not surprise him."

"Let's wait until after six o'clock," Rollison decided, "and see whether Daffodil comes."

"Mr. Grice may have left his office by then."

"We'll take a chance," said Rollison.

It was then twenty minutes past five. For the next half-hour he answered the day's correspondence, but could not free his mind of the disappearance of Daff and the possible connection between this mystery and the murder. Suddenly, he pulled open the drawer of a mahogany filing cabinet, and took out a folder marked FRANKEN.

Among the documents in this were photographs of all five members of the family; the women attractive, the men quite handsome, and with a strong family likeness. He looked at his watch. It was five minutes to six. What should he do if Daffodil Lee did not come at six o'clock?

He knew the answer; he would talk to the police at once; if he didn't, it would be taken as a sign of great weakness. He stood up. It was no use pretending he wasn't; he was very much on edge.

At one minute to six, Jolly came in, and began to put out glasses, bottles of whisky and gin, tonic water and soda. Above the subdued noises that this caused came the sharp ring at the front door bell.

It was six o'clock precisely.

CHAPTER 7

ON THE DOT

"SHE's on the dot!" exclaimed Rollison, unable to keep the exultation out of his voice. "I'll go." He strode into the lounge hall, glancing up at the periscope-type mirror which Jolly had installed many years ago as a safety device. Many strange and nearly as many ill-disposed individuals called on the Toff, and Jolly had wanted to make sure that every caller could be identified before the door was opened. It had become second nature to glance up and to see a dwarf-like image of whoever was standing outside.

Now, no one was.

Jolly, behind Rollison, almost cannoned into him. Rollison pointed at the mirror, and Jolly whispered:

"No one, sir."

"Back way," Rollison said. "Hurry."

Jolly moved off swiftly.

Rollison stood for a few seconds, expecting someone to come in sight, press the bell, and then dart to one side again. The bell did not ring. He heard no footsteps, but soon heard the kitchen door close as Jolly went out. It would take his man fully a minute to cross the courtyard and take the nearest alley to Gresham Terrace, and Rollison was in no mood to wait so long.

The bell did not ring again. The silence was such that he began to believe that he had imagined the first ring. He went forward slowly, still peering up at the mirror. He reached the door. Whoever it was playing the fool—

That theme ran through his mind again: this was all a gigantic hoax.

He went swiftly across to an umbrella stand, and selected a silver-knobbed cane, actually a sword-stick. He took a final glance into the mirror, which still blank. He pulled back the latch, slowly, making no sound, and opened the door with great caution. The only new sound was the hum of traffic, and the snort of a motor-cycle starting off.

Impatiently, he thought: "No one's making a fool of me. I'm making a fool of myself."

He moved forward, glancing right and left, and saw the girl.

She was huddled up in the right-hand corner, back towards him, head resting against her arms which were folded against the wall. It was a peculiar, unnatural position. Because of it the back of her yellow linen skirt was raised several inches above her knees, by no means elegant. Her hair, so daffodil yellow, fell to her shoulders untidily; it looked as if she hadn't brushed or combed it for a long time.

"My God!" breathed Rollison. "She can't be dead."

He heard footsteps on the stairs below, and drew back from the girl, heart in mouth. He peered over the side of the top flight, peering down a well which went down four stories, and caught a glimpse of Jolly.

He went back to the girl.

In a ridiculous way he was almost afraid to touch her, but quite suddenly he gripped her by the waist, and pulled. She was a dead weight. He almost expected her to swing round and laugh at him, head tossed back, but she did not. As he drew her away from the wall her head drooped forward; only the wall had been keeping her upright.

Jolly called from the foot of the flight of stairs.

"Are you all right, sir?"

"Yes. Come up this way." As he spoke, Rollison slid one arm round the girl's waist, the other gently across her breasts, and turned her round. Her face was like wax. It was Daffodil, of course it was Daffodil. She did not seem to be breathing. Her eyes were made-up too heavily with eyeshadow, and there was too much lipstick on her beautifully shaped lips, which were closed.

It was like looking into the face of a dummy.

"Is it—is it a model, sir?" Jolly's voice was just above a whisper.

"Not this time."

"She hardly looks real."

"She feels real," Rollison said. "I doubt if they've

started making dummies with sponge rubber accessories."
He took one arm away, and Daffodil swayed. He supported her again as he went on: "Turn down the spare-room bed."

"At once, sir."

Jolly propped the front door wide open, so that Rollison could carry the girl in. He put an arm beneath her knees and the other round her shoulders and hoisted her. As he did so, a light flashed, almost blinding him.

He glanced down, and saw a little man holding a small camera at his face, grinning, and calling:

"Just one more!"

"Use those pictures and your paper gets no story," Rollison called.

"You can't blackmail the press, Toff," the photographer declared. "What about a full face, cheek to cheek?"

He had already taken a photograph, so there was nothing to be done about that. If the picture was to be used, it might as well be a good one. So Rollison turned 'and posed, not cheek to cheek but not far from it. The flash came again.

"Thanks," said the photographer. "That's what I call turning the other cheek. Who is she?"

"Just say a friend." Rollison turned and went into the flat, pushing the door to with his heel. It closed firmly. He went along the passage to the bedrooms, his own on the left, the spare-room on the right. Jolly had stripped it down to the sheets, and put a car rug over it. As Rollison laid Daffodil down, Jolly took off her green linen shoes. She had nice legs and ankles.

"What do you think the trouble is, sir?"

"It's a question of which drug was used."

"I suppose so. She looks—*very* unreal, sir." Jolly gave the impression that he still doubted whether she was made of flesh and blood.

"She looks very attractive, too," Rollison said. "Fresh as spring."

"The lily has been somewhat gilded," Jolly remarked.

Rollison chuckled, then placed his hand on the girl's forehead, and his thumb on her right eyelid. He opened the eye enough to see the pin-point pupil.

"Morphia," Jolly stated flatly. "Shall I send for Dr. Welling?"

Rollison busied himself, feeling Daffodil's pulse, taking her temperature.

"She's not in a very bad way but it might be a good idea to send for Welling as a precaution."

The front door bell rang again, and they stared at each other, equally apprehensive, remembering what had followed the last ring at that bell.

Rollison forced a laugh.

"If it's the press, I've nothing to say yet."

"I'll get rid of them," said Jolly.

Rollison pulled up a chair, sat down, and took Daffodil's left hand, feeling for the pulse. It wasn't bad, only a little slow. It was now possible to see that she was breathing softly through her nostrils. She looked slim and trim; quite lovely, in fact; and if she had her hair done, she would probably be beautiful.

Jolly came back, obviously perturbed.

"Who?" asked Rollison, still preoccupied.

"Superintendent Grice, sir." Jolly sounded worried.

"Well, well," Rollison said, straightening up. "Mahomet has come to the mountain. Did he say why?"

"No, sir."

"I gather from your manner that his attitude could be improved upon."

"He is somewhat aggressive, I would say."

"Quote him."

Jolly almost smiled. " 'What fool trick is he up to now?' "

"That could be worse," opined Rollison judicially. "It could have been 'What the hell is he playing at?' Put some blankets over our guest, will you?"

Jolly was unfolding fluffy yellow blankets as Rollison went out of the bedroom. He did not go immediately into the big room, but stepped into the bathroom and rinsed his face in cold water. He felt clearer and fresher as he dabbed himself dry, and was bright-eyed when he went to see Superintendent William Grice of New Scotland Yard.

Grice was an old friend, although there had been a time, many years ago, when he had been almost an enemy, and hostile to anything which an amateur detective might attempt. The years had taught them natural respect as well as liking. Nevertheless, there were occasions when the almost inbred prejudice of a policeman towards a private detective revealed itself, if only in impatience and moods of aggressive suspicion. Jolly and Rollison had come to know Grice so well that they knew what mood he was in almost at a glance.

Rollison glanced at his sharp features, the Roman nose rather white where the skin stretched tight across the bridge, otherwise sallow. In fact Grice always looked as if he had come from a long holiday in the sunshine, even when he hadn't been out of England for a year. He had brown hair, going grey, brushed straight back from his forehead, clear brown eyes, a pointed chin. As nearly always, he was dressed in a well-tailored suit of dark brown serge.

"I never did it," Rollison protested.

"So that's the attitude you're going to take, is it?" Grice almost growled.

"Now, Bill." Rollison put out his hand. Grice had a quick grip and a cool palm. "What will you have?"

Grice hesitated, and then said: "A bitter lemon."

"Still on the water wagon?"

"I have been for forty years," Grice said. He watched Rollison pour himself out a whisky and soda, took his bitter lemon, and sipped. "Cheers. What are you playing at, Rolly?"

"Are you thinking of the Madame Tussaud trouble?"

"Yes."

"Then I'm not playing at anything. I'm in earnest."

"Why didn't you talk to me before you began all this?"

Rollison contemplated the Criminal Investigation Department man very thoughtfully, and said reflectively:

"I think we're talking at cross purposes."

"Don't blame me for that."

"What should I have consulted you about? Having a model of me put in the Chamber of Horrors?"

"No. Your reasons for it."

"But the only reason I had was sheer conceit."

"Don't be a fool," Grice said tartly.

"It's true. I might tell you that no amateur detective has been on show at the Exhibition before. It's a considerable distinction."

Grice frowned, hesitated, and then said half-wonderingly:

"You can't be."

"Can't be what?"

"As conceited as that."

"I delete the word conceit, and substitute 'pride'."

"That's even worse."

"To get down to cases, I didn't dislike the idea of being guyed at the Exhibition," Rollison said, soberly. "After the first shock reaction, which was 'no', I decided it wasn't a bad idea."

"You really mean this was originally Madame Tussaud's idea?" Grice was incredulous.

'The old soul's been in her grave for a hundred years or so, but the company approached me. They had a ridiculous idea that the Franken case warranted it." When Grice stared as if in amazement, Rollison went on with mock humility: "I couldn't understand it, but it did become a *cause célèbre* and a lot of misguided people thought I'd brought the chickens home to roost. It's an unfair world, isn't it?"

"It's a damned silly world in some ways," Grice growled. "Well, if you tell me this, I've got to believe it. I wouldn't have from anyone else. Who's playing the fool with your effigy?"

"I'm trying to find out."

"You really don't know?"

"Tell me one thing, and then I'll tell you the whole story," Rollison offered. "Why did you come here?"

Grice rubbed the bridge of his nose.

"And why come in anger?" Rollison added.

"Not anger, just exasperation," Grice corrected. "I thought you'd put the Exhibition up to the Franken/Toff tableau."

"Why on earth should I?"

"To draw the rest of the Frankens," said Grice.

"Oh," mused Rollison. "Light dawns. You think I think the brothers and their sister were involved in the murder, and that I am trying to lure them into indiscretions which will lead to their downfall."

"That's precisely what I think," confirmed Grice. "Look me in the eye, and deny it."

Rollison looked him squarely in the eye. "I deny it," he stated flatly.

Grice tossed down the rest of his drink as if he needed it to sustain himself. Rollison sipped his, and sat on the arm of an easy chair.

"Why don't you sit down?"

"I'm all right," Grice said. "Well, well. Then *why?*"

"I promised to tell you a story," Rollison said. "I really think you should sit down. Another bitter lemon?" Grice shook his head. "Sure? . . . All right, then. The first intimation I had of trouble . . ."

The telling took fifteen minutes, and during it Rollison

realised how much had happened in so short a time. He studied Grice throughout, but it was impossible to guess what was going through the Yard man's mind—until almost the last sentence. Then Grice jumped to his feet, and almost cried out in anguish:

"You mean that girl's still here?"

"Come and see for yourself."

"But she should be seen by a doctor!"

"I was about to send for one when you came," Rollison said.

"Half-an-hour could be important."

"Now don't panic," Rollison cautioned. "She was dosed with morphine."

Grice went into the bedroom and took the girl's wrist.

"Apart from keeping her warm and cosy there's nothing to be done, even if you put her in a hospital," Rollison went on.

Grice put the girl's wrist down, and pulled up her right eyelid. He grunted.

"Hospital's a good idea."

"Why?"

"We can have a policewoman by her side when she wakes."

"Bill," Rollison said quietly. "I don't think you're on the right lines about this. The girl's been drugged with one of the morphine derivatives. It could have been self-administered, or administered with her knowledge, so that she did what I ordered, but couldn't tell me anything. If you take charge of her now I've no chance of dealing with her friends."

"It was you who threatened to go to the police," Grice pointed out sharply.

"I forced an issue. They've met me half-way. Let me take it from there. If it goes too far, I'll tell you." When Grice didn't answer, Rollison picked up the list of the names of the girls in the studio in Conning Square. "Check on these, and let me know if there's any association with the Frankens, will you? If there is, then I know nothing will stop you from taking official action, but it's too early yet."

Grudgingly, Grice answered: "I will, if you send for a doctor to look at that girl."

"Agreed."

Grice drew a sharp breath.

"Rolly."

"Yes?"

"Are you sure this isn't a roundabout way to get the Yard on the trail of the young Frankens?"

"If it is, it's none of my doing," Rollison said. "Thanks for your help, Bill."

Twenty minutes after Grice had gone another visitor arrived; a rather didactic middle-aged locum for Dr. Welling. He examined Daffodil, diagnosed morphine, recommended plenty of blankets, a hot water bottle, and strong, very sweet coffee when she came round.

"If you hadn't told me that the police already knew I I should have to report to them," he stated.

"Why not report, in any case?" asked Rollison. "How long do you think it will be before she's conscious?"

"I cannot say for sure. Several hours, at least. I will be at home, if there should be any emergency." The doctor went off, self-important and almost military in bearing, and Rollison let Jolly show him out.

It was nearly half-past seven.

"What do you propose to do next, sir?" inquired Jolly.

"Eat whatever you've got ready and decide whether to wait in for Liz Bonham or her friends, or whether to go and see them again," said Rollison. "On balance, wait, I think. What would you do?"

"Wait, sir, undoubtedly—at least until the young woman has come round and you have had a chance to talk to her. In view of the warm evening and the possibility of haste, I have prepared a cold collation."

"Just right," said Rollison.

There was in fact game pie, Wiltshire ham, Aylesbury duck, and Scotch beef, in an array so tempting that Rollison almost forgot that he was waiting in a state of considerable tension for a girl to come round, or for some move from her friends.

He had finished a dish of luscious raspberries and Devonshire cream, and was contemplating coffee, when the front door bell began to ring. Whoever was there kept a finger on the bell, and then began to thump on the door so hard that it seemed in danger of falling in.

CHAPTER 8

"ONLY ONE"

"THERE'S only one man there," Jolly said, as if he did not believe it.

"Unless there are others out of sight."

"But he's pressing and banging." Jolly peered up at the tiny reflection in the periscope-type mirror. "Do you know him, sir?"

"Never seen him before in my life."

"Open the door!" roared the young man who was banging and ringing. "I know you're in—open the door!"

"Shall I?" asked Jolly.

"With caution," conceded Rollison.

Jolly slid back the door bolt, which was reverberating under the hammering, and stepped hastily to one side. The young man staggered in as the door yielded to another hammer blow, but he was not using a hammer, only a length of rubber hose. He was fair, powerful looking, somewhere in the late twenties. His cheeks flushed in the way common among people with fair complexions. He had the bluest of blue eyes, which seemed on fire. There was something peculiar about his expression.

He staggered, recovered his balance, glared at Rollison and cried:

"You swine! Where is she?"

"In the bedroom," Rollison answered politely.

"What!"

"The spare bedroom. In bed."

The glittering eyes seemed to burn with even greater intensity, and the young man's lips parted, he raised the hose like a hammer, and cried:

"You admit that she's—"

"Come and see," said Rollison.

In one way, this was a moment of great relief—the moment when Rollison really changed from the defensive to the attack. The young man raised his arm as if to strike, and Rollison snatched at his wrist, twisted, thrust his arm up behind him in a hammer lock, and ran him towards the bedroom.

"That's better," Jolly approved, *sotto voce.* He closed the door and moved sedately in Rollison's wake.

The spare bedroom door was half-open. Rollison pushed the fair-haired young man into it, and it swung back, to show the piled up blankets and Daffodil's face, slightly flushed with the warmth. Rollison let the young man go, pushing him slightly. He fetched up against the foot of a quilted foot-panel, staring down.

"Daff!" he gasped.

"*Daff*odil," he said in a kind of groan.

"Please, Daff. It's Philip." He moved along the bed, hands outstretched towards her, quite forgetful of his violence of a moment before. "Wake up."

The girl did not stir.

As if oblivious of the men behind him, the young man who called himself Philip went down on one knee beside the bed, and placed his hands against the blankets, his fingers interlocked. It was almost as if he were praying—and as if in a moment he would burst into tears.

"Daff," he pleaded.

Rollison was on the point of telling him that the girl would not wake when Philip stiffened, and thrust his face close to Daffodil's. He stayed like that for a moment, then sprang to his feet and swung round. His cheeks as well as his eyes were burning.

"What have you done to her?" he cried. "Tell me what you've done!"

"Don't blame me," said Rollison. "She was sent here like that."

"You're a liar!"

"Philip," Rollison said quite gently, "if you call me a liar again, I will run you out of the flat by the seat of your pants, and you won't come back. Who are you??"

"But—she couldn't have walked here like that."

"Someone carried her. Was it you?"

"No!"

"*Was it you?*"

"Of course it wasn't me. I wouldn't hurt her." The man's voice dropped so low that the next words were barely audible. "I love her too much. What—" his voice strengthened. "What's happened to her?"

"She's been drugged."

Instead of asking the obvious question, Philip asked:

"Is it—dangerous?"

"No. A doctor's seen her, she'll be herself by tomorrow."

"Why—why did she come here?"

"I asked her to come."

"But—she wouldn't do this to herself."

"I hope she wouldn't," said Rollison.

"But it stands to reason!"

"Philip," Rollison said reasoningly, "let's start at the beginning. And we'll leave Daff alone." He led the way out, half-closing the door behind him. Philip went dazedly along the passage into the drawing-room. Jolly appeared at the other door.

"Will you have a drink?" Rollison asked Philip.

"Eh?"

"A drink."

"Oh. Oh, yes, yes please. May I have a whisky?"

"Soda? Or plain water?"

"Eh?" Philip looked bemused.

"Soda, or—"

"Oh, no. Neat."

"Neat?"

"Without anything," Philip insisted.

Rollison motioned resignedly to Jolly, who was at the bottles. He poured out, added soda to Rollison's whisky, and brought both drinks across on a small salver. Philip took the glass nearest him, sniffed at it, then tossed the neat whisky down. In fact he left a third of the glassful. He did not gasp, pause, or look in any way disconcerted by the fire he had thrown down his throat.

"Cheers. Why should you want to see her?"

"I thought she might have information for me."

"What about?"

"Someone keeps blinding me by proxy."

Philip tossed down the rest of his drink.

"Well, *Daff* wouldn't."

"There are a lot of things Daff wouldn't do, according to you. What's your name?"

"Philip Gant."

"What is Daffodil Lee to you?"

"Nothing, except—I mean I wish she was more than a friend."

"So you're just friends?"

"If you must know, I want her to marry me, but she won't."

"Oh," said Rollison, almost weakly. "Someone else in favour?"

"Not as far as I know." Saying that, Philip stiffened. "She's never said so."

"What brought you here?"

"Eh?" As he ejaculated, Philip Gant glanced at the array of bottles and then at his empty glass. "Er—I wonder if I could have the same again?"

As he spoke, Jolly came forward from a spot where he could hear without being seen. He refilled Philip Gant's glass, and retired, watching the young man in fascination.

"Thanks . . . Cheers." Philip gulped the whisky down, "What did you ask?"

"Why did you come here?"

"The girls sent me."

"Norah, Isobel, Mandy and Liz?"

"Mandy wasn't there. They said Daff had had to come and see you. They said—" Philip Gant flushed.

"Yes?"

"They said you'd forced her to come."

"In a way, I had."

"What way?"

"I said if she didn't come I'd send for the police."

"But good God, man—why?"

"She'd disappeared."

"But she's here!"

"She was missing this morning."

"Oh," said Philip, suddenly rather vaguely. "I see. Well, she isn't now."

"Why did you go to see her tonight?"

Philip stared at him, and for the first time Rollison saw his eyes without the flash of fire, and he was surprised, for they were rather vague and almost shallow. Philip moistened his lips, and muttered:

"I try every night."

"Try what?"

"Try to see her."

"Won't she see you?"

"Not—not always."

"How often does she?"

Philip looked utterly dejected as he answered:

"She avoids me deliberately. She—she won't have anything to do with me." His voice was as limp as his eyes were vague. "I thought if I helped her tonight, she might change—"

Rollison interrupted into what was already a pause.

"Philip, do you mean you went along to Conning Place tonight and three of the girls who share a flat with Daff sent you round here because Daff was supposed to be in trouble. Is that it?"

"Eh?"

"Is that what happened? They told you I was holding her here against her will?"

Philip's eyes seemed to glaze over.

"Yes," he said. "I wonder—" he broke off.

"Yes?"

"Could I have—a snifter?"

"Philip," Rollison said, "how many snifters have you had tonight?"

It would not have surprised him had Philip Gant retorted: "None of your business," or something like that. Instead, he looked almost apologetic as he said:

"Several. But—er—I'm not drunk."

"No." Rollison did not elaborate, but poured out whisky himself, and gave it to Philip, who took it eagerly, raised it half-way to his lips, then hesitated, as if he knew he should not drink it too quickly.

"Do you know who I am?" asked Rollison.

"A man."

"Do you know my name?"

"No," answered Philip, and added with great earnestness: "Haven't met before, have we?"

"No," answered Rollison. "Where do you live?"

"Chelsea."

"Do you have a car?"

"Not with me. I—but can't I stay here?"

"Why?"

"To look after Daff."

"We'll do that."

"Oh," said Philip. Again he became rather vague, although he said with great precision: "Thank you. Then I think I'll go now."

"Would you like a lift home?"

"Not going home," said Philip. He looked more vague than he had all the evening. "I'm going to my club."

He nodded, glanced furtively at the bottles, then tossed his drink down. As he went to the door his gait was quite steady, and there was not even the suspicion of a roll. He reach the door just ahead of Jolly, at whom Rollison mouthed:

"Let him try."

Philip opened the door with great care, but without

fumbling. He went out, and Jolly closed the door on him, then turned and hurried out of the hall, without a word. There was no need for a word. He would go back way into Gresham Terrace, and follow Philip Gant.

There wasn't much mystery about the man, Rollison believed. He was not simply drunk, he was a hopeless alcoholic. For a while his rage had broken through the calm façade which he had developed to hide the truth from all but the discerning.

Rollison turned back to the room, hesitated, went along to see Daff, and stood staring at her for several seconds. Then he went into the kitchen and on Jolly's phone, dialled Ebbutt's number. An ex-prize fighter named Wrightson answered him—and Wrightson was exactly the man whom Rollison wanted to speak to.

"Percy, Jolly could do with some help, and we've a young lady guest for a day or two. Can you and your wife—"

"*D*elighted, Mr. Ar!" Wrightson did not allow Rollison time to answer. "My old dutch was only saying this afternoon she could do with a few days up west. When do you want us?"

"This morning," answered the Toff.

"Now, give us a chance, Mr. Ar, we can't—oh, I getcha! Strike a light, you'll give me the splits, that's what you'll do. And I bought it—you wait till I tell my wife."

"Nine o'clock?" asked Rollison.

"On the dot, Mr. Ar."

On the dot—as Daff had been, reflected Rollison when he rang off. It was now a quarter to eight, so he had an hour and a quarter's guard duty here, unless Jolly returned before then. An hour and a quarter wasn't long, but it could seem a very long time indeed. Rollison went into the living-room, contemplated the shoe-lace which had in virtual fact hanged a man and a woman, and speculated. Then he sat at the desk and jotted down a note of all the things that had happened since the first hole in the eye.

One of the remarkable facts was that his visits to Madame Tussaud's seemed a long way off.

Another was that as he called on his memory, a stocky figure dressed like a policeman appeared clearly, although he had forgotten the man when explaining everything to Grice. He had given less thought and attention to that 'policeman' than to anyone else, and that might well be a mistake.

Now, his thoughts began to click with the kind of precision he liked, dovetailing into one another. He scribbled notes, of which a fair copy would have read:

1. A powerful man (or two less powerful) had lifted the ladder out of position at the girl's studio.
2. A powerful man (or two less powerful) had carried Daffodil Lee up the stairs, all four flights of them, to his flat.
3. The 'policeman' had looked a very powerful man indeed.

What Rollison needed next was evidence that the 'policeman' had been in Gresham Terrace at about six o'clock. That was the kind of inquiry which the police could make with a lot of fuss, and Jolly could make with a little luck in a matter of an hour or two. He wrote a brief note to Jolly, and had hardly finished it before Jolly appeared at the front door; he seldom used the back way when working on what he called an investigation.

Rollison heard the door open, and handed Jolly the note.

"That's your job after Percy Wrightson and his wife move in," he said, and added almost without a pause: "How did you get on?"

"Not too badly, sir," said Jolly, in a tone which told Rollison that he had almost certainly done very well. "I followed Captain Gant to the Sky High Club. As you may know, sir," added Jolly smugly, "that is a Services Club, and each member must have been injured in a bomb or mine disposal mission. I understand from the second barman that he is a regular visitor to the club, which is in Victoria, not far from the station in Vauxhall Bridge Road."

"So that's where he drinks," Rollison said, almost sadly.

"He is of course an alcoholic, sir. Apparently it began when a mine on which he was working blew up. No one quite knows how he escaped, but two men with him were killed."

Rollison said grimly: "It looks as if Captain Philip Gant needs a lot of help."

"In more ways than one, sir," agreed Jolly. "According to the second barman, he is going blind."

CHAPTER 9

GOING BLIND

"BLIND!" echoed Rollison.

"Yes, sir. I didn't think it would be long before the significance of that became apparent."

Both of them looked towards the Trophy Wall. Stuck against a book, which had been used by a poisoner to study his method of murder, was the photograph out of which an eye had been burnt; and in both their minds was a picture of the face, with a gaping hole where there should have been an eye.

"Better not jump to conclusions," Rollison said gruffly. "How well did you get on with this second barman?"

"He is amenable to both flattery and bribery, sir."

"Bribe him as much as you have to. We're looking for a man who answers this description." Rollison tapped the note which Jolly was holding, and Jolly opened it and read closely. After a moment he glanced up, and there was suppressed excitement in his eyes.

"A man answering this description was outside here to-night, sir!"

Rollison said sharply: "Are you sure?"

"He was dressed in a policeman's uniform," said Jolly. "I had a word with Sir Roslyn's man, who saw him." Sir Roslyn Jessop lived opposite Number 22a. "He was surprised in one way and yet not in another."

"Don't be cryptic," Rollison reproved.

"He was surprised to see a policeman get out of a car and assist a young woman into this house—yet not surprised, as we live here."

Rollison said softly: "So the pseudo-policeman got another uniform and brought her here. *Very* nice work, Jolly. The car?"

"An old Austin."

"With a big door, to get in and out of easily?"

"Possibly, sir. Sir Roslyn's man suspected that the young woman was drunk."

"Jolly."

"Sir."

"We want that copper."

"We know he was at Conning Square, sir."

66

"Yes. I'm going over there now," Rollison said. "You join me when the Wrightsons turn up, in case I need help."

Jolly murmured diffidently: "I suppose that is the right course, sir."

"Don't you think it is?"

"Captain Gant might yield dividends," suggested Jolly.

"Our alcoholic," Rollison said slowly. In the excitement of knowing that the man he had followed that morning had brought Daffodil here, he had forgotten the significance of Jolly's information—that Gant was going blind. Anything to do with the eyesight affected Rollison, simply because of the holes in the eyes of the model head and photograph. "Yes, he might, but I'm not the man to see him. Nor are you. I'll think about Gant."

"With great respect, sir—"

"You still don't agree."

"No, sir, I do not. I feel that a talk with Gant might be very valuable. It is not likely that he will be able to withstand skilful questioning, and he is so emotionally involved with the young woman that once you make him believe she is in danger, he will talk very freely. I would certainly see him in person."

"H'm," mused Rollison. "But not at the Sky High Club."

"I could watch that establishment, and let you know when he leaves, unless—" Jolly left the sentence in mid-air.

"Unless—" echoed Rollison, eyeing his man intently. "So I am to guess what you're driving at. Unless—I go to his home and have a look round there?"

"Precisely, sir. 27 Mandeville Mews, Chelsea."

Rollison grinned.

"You'll have me in jail yet. All right. What time does Madame Tussaud's close?"

"I think it's quite late but I'm not sure," Jolly said. "Shall I get them on the telephone?"

"See if Catlin's in," said Rollison.

There was an answer from the Exhibition, but Catlin had gone home; so had Mr. Bernard, but Eva the make-up artist was there. She sounded bright but anxious as she said:

"I hoped you would call, Mr. Rollison. Do tell me, is there any news of Daff?"

"She's a bit off colour," Rollison temporised.

"Oh, lor! That means she won't be in tomorrow, and I've a head that ought to be finished—well, it can't be helped. You don't realise how good people are at their job until they're away for a day or two. If you see her, tell her not to worry, though. I'll manage." With hardly a pause, Eva careered on: "But what can I do for you, Mr. Rollison?"

"Do you know a Captain Philip Gant?"

"Do I *know* him? He haunts the place!"

"For Daffodil?"

"Certainly not for me!"

"I shouldn't be so sure. Do you carry spare uniforms at Marylebone Road?"

"Well, it all depends. The models are dressed to fit—that reminds me, Mr. Catlin keeps forgetting to ask you if you've a suit you could spare, one you would like to be seen in. Where was I? Oh yes. Sometimes when we change a figure or take it out of the halls for repairs or renovations, uniforms might be left lying about. I know we've a Field-Marshal's, a Sultan's and a Cossack's—would any of those do?"

"A policeman's would be better."

"Policeman's, policeman's—oh yes, there is one. We once had a wax policeman at the entrance to the Chamber of Horrors but we took it away."

"Why?"

"It wasn't right," said Eva. "We used a figure of a rather stocky Air Vice-Marshal and cut down a police uniform to fit. It looked all wrong for a policeman."

"Where's the uniform?" asked Rollison.

"In the wardrobe room, I suppose."

"Is it easy to make sure?"

"I won't be two shakes of a lamb's tail," Eva promised.

Rollison kept the receiver at his ear while talking to Jolly about a suit for the dummy, and Jolly went into some detail about colour and styles. He was in the middle of recommending the 1961 cutaway with the pointed waistcoat as being the most likely to last, when Eva burst out:

"It's not there!"

"Eva," Rollison said, "will you keep a secret for me?"

"Of course."

"Don't tell anyone about the missing uniform but see if you can find it."

remaining room, the kitchen. This was nearly as large as the living-room, very modern in white and pale blue.

On a shelf by the window which overlooked the mews was a small clay bust of Daffodil, like those at the girl's flat. A good likeness, it was much smaller than the wax head in the bed, yet much more comprehensive. It was really a little figurine, and modelled almost down to the waist, a nude figure, beautifully proportioned.

"I don't think I like Philip Gant," Rollison said aloud.

He began to search the flat, but found nothing to help. There were dozens of snapshots, most with Daffodil in them; in a cocktail dress, in a cotton dress, in swimsuits, in ski-pants, in shorts. She was there playing tennis, at the wheel of a car, on a motor scooter. There was one, an enlargement, which Rollison studied very closely.

It was of five girls. Three he knew—Daff, Liz and Is. The others were probably Norah and Mandy. The portraits were good enough to give a clear identification, and to make sure each impressed itself clearly on his mind. He looked round for a copy, but could not find one. Virtually all he had discovered was Philip Gant's infatuation with Daffodil Lee—and with the bottle.

There were full bottles of whisky in a kitchen cupboard, and in the cupboard of a small cabinet in the living-room. There were bottles in the wardrobe, more under the bed.

Suddenly, the quiet was shattered by the ringing of the telephone bell. The instrument was in the little passage, convenient for all the rooms. It rang on and on. Rollison went close to it, hesitating, then lifted it and spoke in a fair imitation of Gant's voice.

"Who is that?"

"I thought you should know that Captain Gant is on his way home," said Jolly, in his clearest voice. "He should be there in about ten minutes."

"You scared the daylights out of me," said Rollison. "Thanks."

"I will be on hand should you need me," Jolly promised.

Rollison smiled as he rang off. The older he got, the more resourceful Jolly became, and the more he appeared to relish whatever he could do to help Rollison. Rollison moved out of the hall into the bedroom, and frowned at the sight of Daffodil's head in wax on Philip Gant's pillow.

Wishful thinking?

The agonising pretence of a man at the end of his tether?

As these thoughts passed through Rollison's mind, there was a sound outside: of footsteps. It was only two minutes since Jolly had said that Gant would be in in ten. A key scraped in the lock, an unmistakable sound. Rollison backed swiftly behind the bedroom door, squeezing between it and the wardrobe. The front door opened with a brisk-sounding movement, and a man stepped inside and closed the door firmly.

Rollison had a curious feeling that this was not Philip Gant. He could not see but he had heard Gant's footsteps, and these were not familiar. He twisted his neck round and tried to catch a glimpse of the man, but failed. If the man came in here—

He went straight ahead into the living-room.

Rollison ventured cautiously from his hiding place, and went as far as the door. The man coughed, and the sound was not like Gant—it was much deeper.

Who?

The man moved again and Rollison dodged quickly out of sight, but was able to catch a glimpse of him.

It was the pseudo-policeman, beyond any doubt. His square, heavy-featured face was quite unmistakable. He was dark-haired, and needed a shave. He went into the bathroom, without bothering to close the door.

What was he doing with a key to this flat?

Would Gant expect to find him here?

Rollison began to smile, if a little tensely. He would soon find out what the alcoholic captain was expecting, and the meeting between the two men might tell him everything he wanted to know.

Bless Jolly!

The pseudo-policeman came out of the bathroom, and turned towards the bedroom. Rollison caught his breath. The man started to come in, but stopped in the doorway, hidden from Rollison by the door.

"Bloody pervert," he said.

Then footsteps sounded on the cobbles outside, and the pseudo-policeman stepped into the tiny hall. He was certainly not going to conceal himself from Philip Gant.

CHAPTER 10

FACE TO FACE

ANOTHER key grated against the lock. This time there was no crispness, but a wavering kind of scratching, and when at last the door opened, it was slowly—as a drunken man might open it. Footsteps sounded, then there was a swishing sound, and the door slammed.

Rollison stood expectantly.

Gant appeared to draw in a deep breath. Then he gasped:

"What—what—what are you doing here?"

"Waiting for you," the other man replied.

"Who are you?"

"A friend of a friend of yours."

"I don't know what you're—you're talking about."

"You don't have to—provided I know what you're talking about."

There was another pause, which lasted much longer, before Gant said almost shrilly:

"Don't you talk to me like that!"

"I'll talk to you any way it pleases me."

"You—you get out of my house."

"Stop fooling, Gant," the stranger said. "Just tell me what Rollison said about—"

He broke off, his voice rising. There was a flurry of sound, of thuds, of blows, followed by the unmistakable sound of a man falling. Rollison had to force himself to stay out of sight, anxious though he was to see who had won the first round.

The pseudo-policeman spoke in a voice redolent with disgust.

"Get up, you slimy weed." There was no sound. "Get up!" A moment later: "All right, I'll pull you up by your ears, that ought to teach you who's boss."

There was a sharp, squealing gasp, as if he had put his words into action, and Gant was in pain. Scrabbling sounds followed, and a moment later Gant said breathlessly:

"I want a drink."

"You can wait for it."

"Gimme a drink! I must have a drink!"

"You're pickled in alcohol already. Won't you ever learn?"

"*I tell you I must have a drink!*" screeched Gant.

The other man said: "You'll probably talk gibberish if you don't have one." Movements suggested that they were going into the living-room, and Gant seemed to be breathing very heavily. Further away, glass clinked against glass, there was a gurgle of liquid, a gasping. Rollison had a vivid mental picture of Gant tossing neat whisky down his throat. Since then he had been to the Sky High Club; he must be absolutely soused.

"Sit down," the stranger ordered.

Gant was breathing in short, sharp gasps, making enough noise for Rollison to move safely from behind the door and closer to the passage. The living-room door was half-open, and through the crack between door and frame he could see Gant's face, turned away from him and obviously looking at the other man.

"What—what do you want?"

"What did Rollison say to you?"

"Who are you?"

"Concentrate on what I'm saying. What did Rollison say?"

"You've no right here!"

"Listen, Gant," the dark-haired man said in an ominous sounding voice, "I don't want any fooling or wasting time. You're not so sozzled as all that. What did Rollison say?"

"You—you get out of my house."

"Why, you soak!" A hand appeared in front of Gant's face, open, back towards Rollison. It moved swiftly, smacked against Gant's cheek like a pistol shot, moved twice in quick succession: *Slap-slap, slap-slap.* "Now tell me what Rollison said," he grated.

The hand disappeared. Gant's face was very white, even where he had been struck, but his eyes were blazing, as they had been when he had stormed Rollison's flat. He glared, but did not speak. Either he did not really understand, or he was being stubborn for the sake of it.

"I'll ask you just once more," the dark-haired man said. "If you don't answer, I'll break this over your head."

The hand appeared again. On the palm was the figurine of Daffodil Lee, shaking only slightly. Gant stared at it as if there was terror in his heart.

"No! No, don't break her."

"I'll break it into a thousand pieces if you don't tell me what Rollison said to you."

"Please—please don't break her. I'll tell you anything. Please—please let me have her."

Gant's hand appeared, trembling. Rollison, just able to see, wondered whether the dark-haired man would snatch it out of sight. He did not. Gant took it with infinite care, handling it as gently as if it were made of flesh and blood. He stared at it in adoration, and then hugged it to his heart.

"Now—Rollison," said the other man.

"I went—to see Rollison."

"Why?"

"Daff—Daff was there."

"Who told you?"

"Liz."

"Liz who?"

"Liz at the studio . . . Liz . . ."

"Bonham?"

Gant's eyes lit up.

"Yes! Liz Bonham. She said—she said Rollison had told Daff she must go to see him by six o'clock tonight, or he would tell the police she was missing."

"So you went to Rollison's flat. Was Daff there?"

"Yes."

"Was she all right?"

"She was asleep."

"Asleep?"

"I mean, she was drugged."

"What did Rollison say?"

"He kept asking me about—about Daffodil."

"What did you tell him?"

"I—I said I was in love with her."

"Did he ask you about Madame Tussaud's?"

"What?"

"Did he ask why Daffodil was at Madame Tussaud's?"

"No. Good God, no!"

"Did you tell him?"

"No."

"If you're lying—"

"But I'm not lying. I—" there was a pause, and then Gant's voice rose. "How do you know why Daff went there?" Something akin to terror filled his voice. "How do you know?"

"Just say she told me," the stranger said. "And you didn't tell Rollison."

"He didn't ask me!"

"Well, well," said the man who had posed as a policeman. "So he didn't ask you. The great Toff didn't even ask—" the man broke off, and then he roared with laughter, as if this were the most wonderful joke. Perhaps it was, Rollison thought ruefully, but it wouldn't be long before the man whose name he did not know was laughing on the other side of his face.

Gant was glaring up at him, the figurine still clutched to his chest. His tormentor went on laughing, as if he would never stop.

Then, he did an awful thing.

In front of Rollison's eyes, and with Rollison powerless to stop him, he took a knife from his pocket and drove it into Gant's breast, just beneath the figurine and about the position of the heart. It was so totally unexpected that at first it seemed unreal—like a picture in a nightmare. It was the nightmare expression in Gant's eyes and on his face which drove the truth right home.

Gant was dying in front of Rollison's eyes.

His face went tense, as if with pain as well as understanding. His hands tightened about the figurine, and slowly, awfully, relaxed. The little bust of Daffodil slid to one side, as Philip Gant's eyes began to close and his face to pucker.

The figurine fell.

Gant began to droop sideways.

The figurine hit the floor, and smashed, and the pieces flew about and scattered and clattered.

Rollison felt as if an icy wind had chilled his whole body. For a moment he was too numbed to speak or move, yet he kept telling himself that he must move quickly. One part of his mind was paralysed, the other was acutely alive to danger. He was aware of movements in the other room—he could not see anything but the empty chair.

Remember, the man had a knife.

Remember, he was a ruthless murderer.

Rollison drew slowly to one side. The shock was passing, and he was able to assess the situation and the odds. The murderer was moving about. Crunching sounds told Rollison that he was treading on the broken plaster. Rollison had no weapon, and began to look over his shoulder, into the bedroom, for some weapon of attack, but even if one were there he had no time.

The living-room door opened, and the dark-haired man appeared—and saw Rollison on that very instant.

The murder-knife was actually in his hand.

The shock in the other's eyes must have been as great as that in Rollison's when the murder had been committed. In that split second or so of astounded recognition, the murderer was dumbstruck. His mouth gaped, his body sagged, even the hand which held the knife was limp. If he were given a single moment to recover he would be deadly, but in that almost static stance he was helpless.

Rollison said: "I'll have that." He stretched out his hand for the knife, saw the man's fingers flex, and grabbed not the knife but the wrist. He twisted, and the knife dropped. The man made an ineffectual movement, as fear began to drive away the stupefaction, but before it could develop into any kind of threat, Rollison hit him with a clenched fist, first in the stomach, bringing him jerking forward, then under the jaw with such force that the soles of his feet actually left the ground. He toppled backwards, and fell with his head close to Philip Gant's feet. Rollison did not think there was any fear that the man was feigning unconsciousness, so he bent over Gant.

There was a thickening patch of crimson over Gant's white shirt, shiny as well as bright. He lay on one side, knees bent, in a position very like a child's when asleep. He looked so young. Rollison reached for his pulse and felt it, but it was a waste of time. Philip Gant was dead.

Even now it was almost impossible to believe what had happened.

If only he had revealed himself, instead of playing possum. If only the dark-haired man had even begun to suspect a third party's presence murder would never have been committed. It would have been as easy then as later to deal with the man who had posed as a policeman.

Rollison stood up from Gant.

The dead man had assumed a stature he had not shown in life—the stature which had been his, perhaps, when he had been a serving officer before the tragedy which had driven him to drink. A fearless man in that period, risking his life time and time again to dispose of bombs and mines which might otherwise have killed the young and the innocent. Staring down at him, Rollison felt not only a bitter anger towards the murderer, but bitter self-reproach towards himself.

This was his fault.

Gant was his to avenge.

He felt a sense of personal involvement which had been missing before. At the same time there was a sense almost of anti-climax, that he had caught a murderer.

His eye was attracted by a quiver of movement in the unconscious man's arm. He ignored this, as he bent over the man, unbuttoned his coat and dipped into his breast pocket. Now he knew that the murderer had regained consciousness although he made no overt move. Rollison put the wallet aside and ran through the other pockets, found oddments such as a cigarette case, lighter, keys, loose change, handkerchief, a few tickets and a comb. He turned the man roughly onto his side, knowing that any moment there would be an attempt to turn the tables.

He moved slightly.

The man kicked out at him.

Rollison skipped over the outflung leg, and grabbed the ankle. He got a good hold, twisted, and made the man yelp. He pushed the leg upwards and outwards, at great tension, until sweat gathered on the murderer's forehead and upper lip. Then he let him go, and stood over him, while he went through the wallet.

The first thing to interest him was a postcard-sized print of the photograph of the five girls. All five had signed it with their Christian names, and at the foot were the words: *To Ken*.

Ken.

A letter from a woman read:

"Dear Ken,

I keep waiting and waiting but you never trouble to write. I'd rather know the worst than keep on hoping and hoping. Are you coming back to me or not?"

There was no address, and the only clue to the sender's identity was in the signature: Rosie.

Ken was staring up at him.

There were some more snapshots, all of women, and there was a card with several telephone numbers on it. Rollison scanned these—and quite suddenly was very still.

The third of five numbers was the number of Charles Franken's telephone, before he had been hanged.

He must have appeared so absorbed that Ken made another attempt, this time grabbing at his ankle. The clutch was weak, and easily shaken off. Rollison's toe caught the man in the groin, quite accidentally, making him wince. Rollison bent down, hauled him to his feet, leaned him against the wall and then slapped him across the face time and time and time again, with a restrained vigour which somehow revealed his fury. Ken's head lolled from side to side, he began to gasp for breath, to try to fend off the merciless rain of blows.

Rollison stopped.

"I'm asking you just once—why did Daffodil go to Madame Tussaud's?"

Ken's eyes were streaming with tears of pain, his cheeks were beetroot red, he was still gasping for breath. Rollison stood staring down, poker-faced but seething with hatred. Yet he was sufficiently composed to know that the man could not talk in his present state, it would be futile to keep repeating the question.

He swung round, went to the front door, opened it and looked out. By the corner of the mews stood a familiar figure in black, wearing a bowler, and carrying the almost inevitable furled umbrella. Rollison beckoned him, and left the door on the latch before swinging round to the man named Ken.

A few minutes ago, the murderer would have been on his feet. Now he was on the floor, lying on his side, still gasping, and with his knees bent almost into his stomach. Rollison placed a foot on his shoulder and pushed him over on his back.

"When I say just once, I mean just once. Don't make me show how much I hate your guts."

Ken muttered some gibberish.

"Speak up!" roared Rollison.

He heard two things at the same time. Jolly, coming in and closing the door, and this man saying in a high-pitched voice:

"She's going to burn the place down."

Into the silence which followed, Jolly said almost in horror:

"Does he mean Madame Tussaud's, sir?"

Then Jolly looked beyond Rollison and saw not only Ken but also Philip Gant and the blood at his breast, and Jolly was really shocked.

For twenty minutes, Rollison questioned Ken, who said that his surname was King. He did not alter nor add to his story—that Daffodil Lee planned to burn down Madame Tussaud's.

"Don't ask me why, I don't know," growled King.

By then his voice was stronger, he looked more normal, and there was truculence in his manner which seemed to arise out of the depth of his fear. Fear showed in his eyes when Rollison lifted the telephone, and dialled Whitehall 1212.

CHAPTER 11

DEAD HERO

FIRST came the Squad cars, then Divisional police, next a police surgeon and finally, from his home in Putney, Superintendent Grice. By the time he arrived, the mews was choc-a-bloc with cars, policemen, newspapermen, photographers and indignant tenants of the nearby flats, all of whom were questioned when going in and when going out.

The tiny flat was even more crowded, at its fullest when Grice pushed across the bedroom towards Rollison, who was hemmed into a corner. In another corner, with two policemen close to him, was Kenneth King.

"Mind your backs," an ambulance man called out.

Rollison saw a stretcher being carried past the door. Grice ignored that as he stood in front of King.

"You understand the gravity of the charge, don't you?" Grice was sharp-voiced.

"No comment," said King.

"Have you anything to say?"

"No comment." The truculence was even more noticeable.

Grice said to the policemen: "Take him into the hall. Division will look after him."

"I've got a question," King said.

"What question?"

King looked straight at Rollison, curled his lips, and said in a kind of sneer:

"Ask Rollison what he was doing in the house . . . and

how he can prove he didn't stand by and watch, because it was what he wanted."

"Come on." A constable pulled the arrested man into the passage, where plainclothes men from the Division took over. More "Mind your backs," and "Clear a way there" echoed back into the house. Photographers and fingerprint men had finished, scurrying as Grice stood with obvious impatience, waiting for them to go. At last the two men were in the room together, alone.

"Well?" said Grice.

"I can't prove a thing." Rollison admitted.

"I didn't think you could."

"But I can state on oath that I saw King kill Gant, although I was unable to stop him."

After a pause, Grice said: "Can you state on oath that you had any right to be here in the first place?"

It was a good question, and it created problems. Of course, Rollison could say 'Yes', and claim that Gant had given him permission and a key. A lie in a good cause was hardly unforgivable, but lying for its own sake was never satisfactory. In any case, Grice wouldn't believe him; his expression and the sound of his voice made that clear.

"No," Rollison said.

"No what?"

"I can't state on oath that I had any legal right here."

"How did you get in?" When Rollison simply stared at him, Grice went on with a half smile: "I can't use what you say, and you know it. I'm alone with you and I'd need a third party to turn this into evidence."

"Thanks, Bill," Rollison said. "I just wanted to be sure we were looking at the situation from the same angle. I forced the lock."

"Why?"

"I thought Philip Gant might be in danger."

Grice said drily: "Danger from you?"

"Just danger."

"Rolly," Grice said, suddenly more relaxed, "don't push me or the Yard too far. And don't let Kenneth King get a stranglehold on you. He'll tell his lawyer you were here first, and we may have to take official notice of it. You see the danger as well as I do."

"I see the danger only too clearly," agreed Rollison. "I was an eye-witness. King could state that I was an accessory, and it would be my word against his. Has he named his solicitor yet?"

"No."

"Let me know when he does," Rollison said.

"Rolly," Grice said again, "I didn't like his manner. He seemed far too sure of himself. What's this about his statement that Daffodil Lee plans to burn down Madame Tussaud's?"

"Did he tell you that?"

"He told the Divisional man in charge before I got here."

"It's what he told me, too."

"I'll have to follow it up," said Grice. "Is she still at the flat?"

It would be so easy to say 'Yes'.

It would be so easy to make sure that the police went to his flat, and took her away, or else left a policeman in the bedroom with her. It would virtually mean washing his hands of the whole affair, and Rollison was sorely tempted to do just that. Now that murder was done, there was no telling what grave turn this case might take next.

"Is she?" insisted Grice.

Rollison said: "Yes. But I would like to talk to her, Bill. All you've got against her is the statement of a killer. There's no need for you to take any action against Daffodil Lee yet."

After a long, steady scrutiny, Grice said: "Don't let her leave London. I want to talk to her."

"Thanks, Bill." Rollison spoke with real feeling. "I won't forget that. What do you want from me now?"

"A statement of what you saw here, and what you know about Philip Gant," Grice said. "I'll get a man to take it down and you can sign the statement in the morning."

It was after eleven o'clock before Rollison reached Gresham Terrace. The front room light was on, a reliable sign that Jolly was in and waiting up for him. Several men were standing about the entrance to Number 22, newspapermen with their inevitable, interminable questions. It was one of the evenings when it was a strain to be affable, and hard to remember that they were only doing their job.

Jolly had the door open when Rollison reached the

landing. Percy Wrightson, who looked as if he was made of dried leather, put his head round the door.

"All okay, Mr. Ar?"

"We're doing fine," Rollison answered.

"*Are* we, sir?" inquired Jolly, a minute later, when Wrightson had gone to the kitchen.

"I don't know yet," said Rollison. "What's on your mind?"

"A most uneasy feeling, sir."

"About the case?" What else would Jolly mean, anyhow?

"Yes," said Jolly. "I feel that—" he waved his hands, as if hopelessly, and it was not often that Jolly was at a loss for words. Rollison waited, perhaps more tensely than the situation warranted.

Jolly went on at last: "I feel that what has happened up to now is a form of hoax which is simply an indication of what is to come. I know I'm not making myself very clear, sir, but I suppose I fear that one hoax will lead to another, each one more dangerous. For instance—" Jolly paused again but Rollison did not interrupt. "You actually saw Captain Gant killed, didn't you?"

Rollison nodded.

"Could it be twisted round in such a way that it might appear that you killed him?"

Rollison felt as if a cold hand was gripping the back of his neck.

"Grice asked practically the same thing," he said. "So it's as obvious as that. No, it can't be!" he added explosively. He swung round to the corner cupboard, took out whisky, poured some into two glasses, and said: "Help yourself to soda."

"Thank you, sir." This was one of the moments when the relationship between Rollison and his man became that of friendship; when it seemed right that they should drink together, right for Jolly to sit back in an easy chair while Rollison squatted on a corner of his desk—his back to the Trophy Wall, and within arm's reach of the shoe-lace which had hanged the Frankens.

Rollison sipped.

"Do you know what you're saying?"

"What do you think I'm saying, sir?"

"That King knew I was at Mandeville Mews, knew what would happen, and killed Gant knowing he could switch the situation to make it look as if I was the murderer." When Jolly didn't respond, Rollison went on sharply: "*Is* that what you think?"

"I wouldn't go so far as to say that," said Jolly. "But the possibility has crossed my mind."

"That I was lured to Gant's place?"

"Yes, sir."

Rollison took a deeper drink, and said: "I don't believe it."

"I certainly hope you're right not to."

"Have you seen Miss Lee since you returned?"

"She's still sleeping."

"What time do you think she'll come round?"

"I would have thought any time now," Jolly said.

Rollison nodded, and went into the spare bedroom. He could hear Percy Wrightson talking in undertones to his wife, from a tiny extra room close to Jolly's, but there was no sound from the girl who lay so still.

Rollison stood looking down on her in the soft light of a bedside lamp. She hardly seemed to be breathing, she lay so motionless. She was so young and pretty, so much like her name, but she hardly seemed real. Rollison suddenly felt a sharp, new fear:

Daffodil Lee looked as if she were made of wax.

He held his breath for a few moments, staring. *Was* she breathing? She was, of course she was! Yet he turned, picked up a silver-backed hand mirror, and held it in front of her lips. He could hardly wait to draw it away and look at the glass.

It was misted where her lips had been, yet for a few moments he had almost dreaded that he would find her dead.

Jolly was in the doorway.

"Jolly."

"Sir?"

"Someone must stay in the room with her."

"I've arranged for Percy to take a turn, sir, and Mrs. Wrightson says she is always up by six o'clock, so that will be two hours each. Which spell will you take?"

Rollison said: "The second, Jolly. You take the first."

"Very good, sir."

Rollison looked again at the unconscious girl. Her dress was off and her clothes had been loosened; Mrs. Wrightson would no doubt slip her into a nightdress. Rollison left the bedroom. It was impossible to explain or to express his fears, but they were very real. There was another fact, too; the sense of being in a kind of mental strait-jacket seemed to get worse. It was as if his actions were being controlled by pressure outside himself. It was easy to dismiss the idea as nonsense, but that was exactly how he felt. Usually he could be sure of dropping off to sleep, but tonight he was restless, and began to toss and turn. When he did drop off, he had a hazy kind of dream about a group of attractive girls. That faded, and he slept deeply, until he heard a voice.

"Morning, Mr. Ar!"

Morning? And who was waking him?

"Time to get up. If you stay there any longer the sun will be so hot it will burn your eyes out."

Rollison repressed a shudder; Wrightson was the last man to wake anybody, it was like being called by a screeching hen. But here was Wrightson, wearing a white jacket, morning tea tray in his hand, the newspapers tucked underneath one arm, his face cracked in smiles. Then the truth dawned on Rollison.

"Why didn't Jolly call me?" He felt angry as he sat up.

"We decided to take three hours' duty each, wanted you to be in fighting trim for today, Mr. Ar. Going to be a busy day. You wait till you see the papers. Got your picture in them again, you're as photogenic as a Hollywood idol, you are." During this speech Wrightson was putting the tray and the papers down. "Jolly's asleep. My old woman's with the girl."

Rollison said: "How is she?"

"Never better, Mr. Ar!"

"And the girl?"

"Still asleep."

Rollison echoed slowly: "*Still* asleep?"

"Like a babe. Pretty as a picture, ain't she?"

"Yes," said Rollison. "I'll go in and see her in five minutes."

"O.K., Mr. Ar. And I'll run your bath." Wrightson mock-saluted, and went out.

Wrightson liked to pretend that he could out-Jolly Jolly, and there were times when Rollison would have been amused by this demonstration of efficiency. Instead, he wasn't even slightly amused. Two papers had his photograph in, as well as King's, and all of them had a picture of Philip Gant. Only the bare facts of the murder were given so far, and he was hardly mentioned in the text.

After one cup of tea, he pulled on a dressing-gown, and

went into the spare room. There was a faint sound now: *click-click-click-click* of Mrs. Wrightson's knitting needles. She sat in a chair, her feet up, a magazine propped up, reading and knitting with remarkable speed and facility.

Daffodil was lying on her right side, in a nightdress taken from a wardrobe stocked for emergencies. Her clothes were neatly folded over a chair, her handbag stood on the seat, her shoes underneath. Last night she had been left on her left side. She was so motionless that Rollison felt that creeping fear again—that she was dead.

"She's breathing all right," Mrs. Wrightson said briskly. "I make sure every half hour. Must have had a strong dose, mustn't she?"

"Yes, mustn't she," Rollison said grimly. "How often has she moved?"

"Turned over twice, that's all."

Rollison grunted, and tried Daffodil's eyes again. The pupils were as tiny as ever. He released the eyelid gently, watched by Mrs. Wrightson, who had stopped reading but whose needles were *click-click-clicking* all the time.

"She's okay, isn't she?"

"I hope so," Rollison said. "I'll get the doctor to see her again."

This time, the *locum* was less formal, and in fact was obviously puzzled if not perturbed. He took a specimen of Daffodil's blood, and checked her blood pressure, used a stethoscope with a pretentious air of thoroughness, and said finally that he couldn't make it out.

"She should be round," he stated. "If she had enough morphine to put her out for as long as this you'd think she would have suffered acute morphine poisoning. Peculiar, most peculiar. Looks almost as if she were made of wax, doesn't she? I'll get all these things checked, and if she isn't soon round, we'll have to move her to hospital."

"Bill," said Rollison into the telephone. "I think you'd better send an ambulance and collect Daffodil Lee." He explained enough to make Grice understand what had happened, as well as enough of the girl's symptoms to make Grice act at once. That was at nine o'clock. By ten minutes past Daffodil Lee was being carried out of the flat on a stretcher still unconscious. Grice wasn't there himself; a Chief Inspector whom Rollison knew slightly was very non-committal.

"Now what are you going to do, Mr. Ar?" asked Wrightson.

"I'm going to have breakfast," answered Rollison. "Then I'm going to see Daffodil's girl friends."

At a quarter past ten, he stepped into the hallway of Number 47 Conning Square. The symbols instead of the names had acquired a kind of significance he had not thought of the previous morning. No one was about. He went up to the top floor, and found the door closed. There was a limit to what Grice could allow him to get away with, and if he forced another door he might really be in trouble.

He rang the bell, and heard the ringing inside, but could not hear anyone approach. There was no response to a second, third and fourth ring. He tried the handle, but the door was locked. The temptation to force it became almost irresistible, and he probably would have tried but for a sound on the staircase behind him. He tensed himself as he turned round.

A little old woman was coming up the stairs, walking with some difficulty, and gripping the balustrade at every step.

"They're not in," she announced, in a puzzled, even a worried voice. "They weren't here last night, either, they haven't slept here. I don't understand it. I really don't." She sounded slightly querulous, and her wizened face and bony figure strengthened that impression. "Are you a friend of theirs?"

"I know them," Rollison said. "Have you a key?"

"Of course I've got a key, what do you think I'm the caretaker for if I haven't got a key?" She took it out of the pocket of a flowered apron, pushed past him and inserted the key. As she opened the door of the now familiar room, she raised her voice. "Is anyone home yet? Is anyone home?"

There was no answer.

The little old woman walked towards the bedrooms and the attic studio. Rollison could see that the bedroom doors were wide open. He saw the caretaker glance in, then saw her start, clutch at her breast, and stare into the room on the right.

"They're back," she said in a cracked voice. "But they look so funny." In a hoarse whisper she went on: "They look as if they're dead."

CHAPTER 12

FOUR PRETTY HEADS

ROLLISON stood with the old woman in front of him, staring over her shoulder. Two beds were directly in his line of vision, and on the pillows were two pretty heads—Liz Bonham's and Isobel Allington's; Liz and Is.

They did not move.

Rollison went ahead of the caretaker, and looked into the other bedroom. Mandy Fitzherbert and Norah Thomas were there.

But were they?

"They look as if they're dead," the old woman breathed again.

"They don't look real," said Rollison. He went forward, suspicion growing stronger with every step. He bent over Liz's head, and by that time was sure of the truth. He put down his hands and took 'Liz' gently between his hands and lifted. The head, of wax, came off the pillow.

The old woman screamed: "Her head's come off!"

Rollison let the head fall, and swung round in time to stop her from rushing out of the room. In a way it was good to have something to do, in pacifying her and making her realise that this was a kind of sick joke. He helped her to a chair and then went into the kitchen and put on a kettle. Then he went back to the old woman, who was looking better, and no longer muttering to herself.

"When did you come in here before?" asked Rollison.

"About an hour ago."

"Did you look in the bedrooms?"

"Of course I did."

"And weren't the heads there?"

"What do you take me for, young man?" demanded the caretaker. "If I'd seen them before I wouldn't have been so upset, would I?"

"I suppose not," agreed Rollison, sounding abashed. "Did you hear anyone come up?"

"I heard you."

"Before me."

"No, I didn't."

"Do you always hear when people come upstairs?"

"Not if I'm at the back—but I was listening out this

morning." The little eyes became almost suspiciously bright. "How am I to know you didn't come and put those heads there, scaring the wits out of an old body like me?"

"But I haven't had time."

"It wouldn't have taken a minute."

"No," conceded Rollison slowly. He began to smile. "It certainly wouldn't. Would you like a cup of coffee?"

"If it's good," she said.

"I'll make it myself."

"Making yourself at home here, aren't you?"

Her mind, like her eyes, was as sharp as needles. Suspicion glittered in them as she made that comment, but Rollison only grinned as he went back to the kitchen. When he went to see her again, she had gone. He put the two cups of coffee down, and hurried to the ladder, which was back in position. He went up quickly. There were different paintings on the easels, and no sign of the two sketches of himself. He moved towards the modelling stand and searched about, looking for any signs of wax; he saw none. He looked in every nook and cranny until he was sure that no wax had been used up here for some time, but under a canvas in one corner he found a flat box.

Inside was human hair, packed in a plastic bag.

He took out several strands of this, and carried it into the bedrooms. This hair was nearly identical to that in Isobel Allington's head. He pulled several strands from that head and with finicky care tied them into a knot, put them into an envelope with hair from the box, and went back to the ladder.

No one had moved it this time.

As he went down, he heard the old woman saying:

"Well, I don't think he'd got any right here, *I* didn't ask him in. And I'm sure it's the man in the paper."

"We'll soon see," a man said in a deep voice.

Rollison reached the doorway leading to the landing as the old caretaker entered, with a tall, very lean, youthful looking policeman. This policeman seemed more unreal than the man now in a police cell—if he wasn't already in dock, being charged as Philip Gant's murderer.

"There he is!" exclaimed the caretaker.

The lanky policeman stared.

"So I see," he said. "Mr. Rollison, isn't it?"

"Yes," said Rollison.

"This lady has lodged a complaint against you, sir."

"So I did!" the old woman said spitefully. "Going about frightening the wits out of an old woman."

"That's if she had any wits left," remarked Rollison. "Will you let Superintendent Grice know about this as soon as possible?"

"About the heads in the beds?"

"Yes. And I'd like to take one away with me to see if it was made where I think it was."

"I'd rather you left all the heads here, sir." The constable stepped forward, far enough to see the models. His expression changed only very slightly. "In fact as this lady has complained I would rather you stayed until I've had instructions—I'll have to work through my Division, of course."

"I don't want to lose any time," Rollison said. "I'll be back at my flat at one o'clock or I'll tell the Yard where to find me. Are you new on this beat?"

"Not exactly—I've been here about nine months."

"Do you know the tenants here?"

"Know of them—who doesn't?" The constable, a very human young man, persisted. "If you'll just wait until I've talked to my sergeant, sir . . ."

He talked by telephone from the flat, while the caretaker glowered and Rollison listened while letting thoughts and reflections pass through his mind. Most of the time he was aware of the old woman's sharp gaze, until he glanced up and she began to tidy up the big room.

The policeman hung up.

"It's all right for you to go, sir."

"Oh. Thanks."

"But I tell you it's the man whose picture was in the paper," the caretaker protested. "One law for the rich and one for the poor, that's the truth of it."

Rollison fled.

Half-an-hour later he stepped out of a taxi outside Madame Tussaud's, went into Allsop Place, and entered by the door leading to the workshop and offices. There was no one about to stop or question him, and as he went up the narrow stairway, he heard no sound until a bell rang; almost immediately Bernard Tussaud answered.

"No, nothing more to say." He sounded half-vexed, half-tolerant. "And don't put any more of these calls through to me." He placed the receiver down and then said to someone whom Rollison could not see: "Have you any idea when Jim will be back?"

"He said by two o'clock." That was the make-up expert, Eva.

"I suppose he can't be in two places at once," said Bernard. "But I hope he doesn't want to spend too much time with Rollison."

Rollison, about to reveal himself, stayed where he was.

"It's the detective in him," said Eva. After a pause she went on: "At least we've got all the staff we want, for a change, but they looked a tough lot."

That meant that Ebbutt's men had arrived.

"Well, I'll go and see if I can get the Toff's hair started at last," Eva went on. "At least there's been no damage to *this* head." She came out of the room, turned towards the stairs leading to the Exhibition and the workshop, then spun round, having seen Rollison out of the corner of her eye. "Oh! You scared me!"

"Sorry," said Rollison, pleasantly. "But Bernard did give me the freedom of the place."

"Oh, I'm not blaming you. Coming down?"

"Soon."

She smiled, nodded, started off again, and then swung round for the second time.

"Have you seen Daff?"

"Not lately," Rollison dissembled.

"I know one thing, all this is going to postpone the Frankens and you by a month," stated Eva. She went off, moving easily and gracefully, short skirt swirling about her nice legs.

Rollison went into the modelling room. Busts of a Cabinet Minister and a Russian astronaut were on two pedestals, with photographs pinned up on boards close to them. A sculptor was working on each—a middle-aged man and a woman about Eva's age. They had worked through the conversation and even when Rollison spoke they did not glance round.

"Good morning, Mr. Rollison," said Bernard. "You know my brother and Miss Deacon, don't you?" The couple broke off long enough to smile and murmur 'hallo' before turning back and working on the clay figures with infinite patience. "What can I do for you that Jim Catlin can't?" Bernard asked.

Rollison omitted to say that he had no idea what Catlin was doing.

"How long does it take to make one of those clay models?"

"Three or four weeks," answered Bernard Tussaud.

"And there isn't any quicker way than making a cast the way you did mine?"

"That's right."

"Could Daffodil have made wax casts?" asked Rollison.

"Well—" Bernard pursed his lips—"I suppose she could."

"How long would it take?"

Bernard was frowning.

"Jim Catlin could tell you all this just as well as I could," he said, but proceeded to answer: "First the cast, then the plaster, then more wax—well, to allow time for hardening and colouring—would they have hair?"

"Yes."

"The hair would be the longest—say four weeks."

"For each?"

"If one person was making them all, yes."

"And four weeks for the lot if four people were doing one each."

"That's right. Mr. Rollison, why are you asking these particular questions."

"The police will soon be asking you about some heads they've found at Daffodil's flat," Rollison said. "Get all the details from them. Mr. Tussaud, did you know Daffodil Lee before she applied for work here?"

"No."

"Do you know of anyone who might want to burn the Exhibition down?"

Bernard stared. The sculptors stopped working at last, and turned to look at Rollison. There was a strange, almost a tense silence, and in it Rollison could hear the sound of his own breathing and the beating of his heart.

Then Bernard asked: "Why do you ask that?"

"I've been told of a man who says there's danger of arson." Rollison looked from one to the other and was quite sure there was consternation in their minds—consternation at a secret shared. In another room a telephone bell rang on a muted note, and went on and on. "Did you know?"

"Fire is the one thing above all other things that we fear," replied Bernard Tussaud. "It could be absolutely disastrous, even on a small scale. And only this morning a man telephoned me and said that if we used your statue, he was going to burn the place down."

After a long pause, Rollison said: "Do you know who threatened to do that?"

"It was just a man on the telephone. Naturally he didn't give his name. In fact we had decided to wait until we heard what you said about it before going to the police." Bernard was frowning. "There's something I don't quite understand."

"There's a lot I don't understand at all," Rollison said, feelingly. "How could I say anything until I knew about the message."

"But surely—" the other Tussaud said, and stopped short.

"Mr. Rollison," said Bernard, "haven't you seen Jim Catlin this morning?"

"No."

"He was to come and tell you about this."

"I left my flat at a quarter to ten—" began Rollison. He found himself thinking as he spoke that Jolly had known where to find him, that Catlin could easily have caught him up at Conning Place. Why hadn't he?

"Jim left here before nine," said Bernard.

"Didn't he arrive?" the woman sculptor said.

"He must have!" exclaimed the other Tussaud.

"Let me use your telephone," said Rollison gruffly.

"I can't believe it!" Eva was in the corner of the big workroom. "He told me he would be at your flat by half-past nine at the latest. You say you've just spoken to your man, and Jim's not been there at all? It doesn't make sense."

"It didn't seem like Jim to be away so long," remarked Bernard Tussaud. "There's one obvious possibility before we start to panic, though."

"But he's missing!" cried Eva.

"He may have gone off on some chase of his own."

"He wouldn't be such a fool!" Eva turned sharply, caught her arm on a head which stood on a small pedestal behind her, and accidentally swung it round. As a result, Rollison stared at a likeness of himself, one which seemed complete, the eyes as perfect and undamaged as the rest of the model. There was just one startling thing; he was completely bald. Eva grabbed the head. "I couldn't bear it if I were to knock it over, it would be the last straw. There's something evil going on. Damage to the Toff; threats of setting the place on fire, Daffodil missing, and her boy-friend murdered—and now Jim. It's absolutely awful."

"Nothing's happened to Jim yet," Bernard Tussaud protested. "I wish—"

He broke off, as a man in a long white coat came agitatedly to the door, saying to someone out of sight:

"Yes, this way. I'm awfully sorry," he went on to Bernard, "but these gentlemen said they must see you right away."

A tall man came in behind him, carrying a wax head of Is for Isobel. This was Grice's second-in-command, Chief Inspector Fox. Another followed, bearing Norah Thomas's dark head. Two uniformed police followed, carrying a head apiece. They filed into the room, Fox watching Bernard and Eva closely, apparently oblivious of the Toff.

"What we would like to know," he said, "is whether these models were made here." Without looking at Rollison, he went on: "Have you told Mr. Tussaud about them, Mr. Rollison?"

"More or less."

"So this is why you wanted to know how long it would take to make four heads." Bernard looked preoccupied but calm, completely unshakable. "Place them on the bench, please. Eva, will you . . ."

He talked and gave instructions as the heads were placed on the bench, two on each side of Rollison's.

" . . . the lights," Bernard was saying, and Eva switched on the lights so that the faces all showed up vividly. They were too highly coloured to be quite natural despite the fact that each was startlingly life-like. "Well, Eva, what do you think?"

Four policemen, Bernard, Rollison and Eva stood looking at the line of heads.

"No," stated Eva.

"I agree with you," said Bernard. "No, Inspector, those heads were not made here. The wax is slightly darker and of a different mixture . . . the shape and size of the bases are different from any we have. They are very well done indeed, by a very good craftsman, but I would be prepared to stake my reputation on the fact that they were not made here."

"So would I," declared Eva.

"Mr. Rollison," said Chief Inspector Fox, "have you any idea where these were made?" He spoke almost accusingly, as if he felt sure that if Rollison answered truthfully, he would have to answer 'Yes.'

"Not yet," said Rollison, and before anyone could comment, he went on: "There are a lot of things that none of us knows. Mr. Tussaud, when you received the threat to burn down the Exhibition, what else was said?"

"What's this?" Fox was shaken out of his calm.

"I had the threat by telephone this morning," Bernard told him. "As a matter of fact, Mr. Rollison, the man simply said that if we put your likeness *and* that of the F nkens in the Exhibition, the whole place would be burned down."

CHAPTER 13

FIVE MISSING

AFTER a long pause, Fox said clearly: "So somebody doesn't like you, Mr. Rollison," in a tone and with an expression which seemed to say: 'And that I can well understand.' "What special fire precautions are you taking, Mr. Tussaud?"

"We take every possible precaution," Bernard answered. "Even more than we have to by the Council's regulations."

"Are you saying that you don't take this threat very seriously?"

"I take it very seriously indeed," said Bernard. "But I have every confidence that a fire would be quickly discovered and put out."

Rollison watched them.

There was something in Fox's manner which he did not fully understand, a kind of hostility unusual in anyone from the Yard. That wasn't his chief concern. Kenneth King had said that Daffodil meant to burn the place down, and that pointed to a danger it would be easy to underrate—the danger of a fire being started by someone inside, who would know how to prevent it being discovered too soon.

That wasn't all.

He asked mildly: "Have you found the four girls, Inspector?"

"No."

"What four girls?" asked Eva quickly.

"Daffodil's attic-mates."

"Do you mean they're missing, too?"

"*And* Jim Catlin?" Bernard said almost with a sigh.

"What this about Catlin?" asked Fox sharply.

"You tell him, Mr. Tussaud," Rollison pleaded. "I'll be at my flat."

He would not have been surprised had the Yard man tried to stop him, but no one did. He went out of the workshop, knowing that everyone in sight was staring at him. He found his way easily to the Grand Hall, which was thronged with visitors. The atmosphere changed completely. People were talking, a child was crying, a big crowd was gathered about a figure of the latest royal baby. The slow-moving groups went on, all obviously impressed.

Then Rollison saw Bill Ebbutt.

Ebbutt was in an attendant's uniform which was too small for him, but which he had somehow managed to button. He was half-a-head taller than most people in the crowd, exactly the right stature for a security officer. As Rollison drew near him he winked but gave no other sign of recognition. Rollison paused just in front of him, and whispered:

"Main danger could be fire."

"Very good," Ebbutt said.

Rollison went to each of the Halls. Near the tableau of the execution of Mary Queen of Scots one of Ebbutt's men was standing as if fascinated by the scene, and another was near Joan of Arc. In the Hall of Kings, yet another of Ebbutt's men was explaining to an enthralled group of teenagers that Henry VIII was just as promiscuous as he had been painted, and that in addition to his wives he was believed to have had many concubines. Downstairs at the entrance to the Chamber of Horrors, two of Ebbutt's men stood with the stillness of statues. All of them saw Rollison but none gave any sign of recognition. A doorman said:

"Everything all right now, Mr. Rollison?"

"It's improving," Rollison replied.

Four girls and one man missing . . .

"But missing is too strong a word yet," Rollison argued with Jolly, when he reached his flat. "Catlin didn't show up here, did he?"

"No, sir," said Jolly. He looked more grave than

thoughtful as he went on: "I don't think I can recall such an affair as this. It doesn't seem to matter whom you want to question, they disappear in one way or another. Gant is murdered, King arrested, Miss Lee is drugged, the others vanish into thin air."

"Or disappear as if they were wax figures, melted down," said Rollison wryly. "Jolly, I want you to go over to Madame Tussaud's and get a specimen of all the dark hair they use on the heads. Then take 'em all to this—" he took out the envelope in which he had put the hairs from Norah Thomas's model—"to Henri's. Henri will be able to tell us if all the hairs are the same. That way we'll know if any hair was used from Madame Tussaud's."

"Shall I go at once?" asked Jolly.

"Yes."

"Have we any idea whether any of the missing girls are related to the Frankens?" asked Jolly.

"If Grice knows he hasn't let on," answered Rollison. "Grice is being very careful and Fox is being awkward." Rollison stood staring at the shoe-lace on the Trophy Wall. "Almost as if something has happened to make the Yard think there's some kind of a case against me. Jolly—"

"Sir?"

"If you were a Franken, what would you like to happen to me?"

Very quietly, Jolly said: "A hanging, sir."

"Precisely. And the snag?"

"It is too obvious, surely."

"That's what I think. Jolly, get those hairs, take 'em to Henri, and telephone me when you're there. I'll go and see him about them. When you're through, go back to the Exhibition and tell Ebbutt to have his chaps look out for anyone who's joined the staff since the Franken sentence."

"Won't the records show that, sir?"

"I'll look at the payroll," said Rollison. "But let's check two ways."

Two hours later, he walked along Harold Square, one of the smaller and more attractive Georgian squares with a garden in the middle, to a house which was a hundred and fifty years old. It was painted black and white, a home suitable for a duchess or a diplomat. Only one word on a brass plate bertayed the fact that it was not a private house. The word was: *Henri's*.

Rollison had to ring.

A girl who might have modelled for Dior or Hartnell, beautifully made-up and coiffured, opened the door, welcomed him courteously, and betrayed interest only by the faintest inflection in her voice when he gave his name.

"M'sieu Henri is expecting you, Mr. Rollison."

Henri was tall, grey-haired, austere-looking, aristocratic-looking. He was said to be one of the three finest coiffeurs in the world, sharing first place with Antogini of New York and Jenkins of Paris. His offices had some porcelain heads, all be-wigged, and some hair treatments and toupees in a magnificent Regency show case. On his desk were three pieces of white paper, about eighteen inches long, marked A, B and C. On each sheet were a few strands of hair. Henri's face lit up at the sight of Rollison. They shook hands, spent two minutes talking about a world becoming sane, and then Henri said:

"But you did not come only to talk, Mr. Rollison."

"I came to listen."

"You are very gracious." Henri looked at the three lots of hair. "The first, I understand, came from one place." It came from Madame Tussaud's. "It is Rumanian hair, almost certainly from the southern district, and is coarser than the other two samples, which are identical in colour, weight and texture. They are Northern Italian hair, from the Po Valley. The age of the persons from whom the hair was cut would be approximately the same, eighteen or nineteen. Novices, of course, of an Order which demands short hair."

Rollison said: "Wonderful, Henri."

"No questions?"

"Do you expect me to argue with you?"

"No. But there are some questions you could ask."

Rollison grinned. "Where in England would I be able to get this particular hair?"

"It so happens that I know that the first comes from Madame Tussaud's; they had a Rumanian consignment in a few weeks ago. The other—" Henri hesitated, as if to whet Rollison's appetite. When Rollison did not speak, the Frenchman went on: "Cottrell's probably, of Knightsbridge. I needed some Italian hair of similar texture to make a toupee for a patron, and obtained some from Cottrell's. They have good contracts in that part of Italy."

"Henri," Rollison said, "you ought to become a policeman. Whom shall I see at Cottrell's?"

"Jameson Cottrell himself," Henri answered. "I will tell him to expect you."

No one could be in any doubt about Cottrell's. It was in a narrow turning off Brompton Road, near Harrods, and the shop window was filled with heads and wigs and combs and shampoos, and assurances that *ici* one speaks most European languages. Women under driers were visible through partly open doors and half-drawn curtains. Rollison was led by a perfumed tomboy with a mass of red curls up a flight of narrow stairs to an office scarcely large enough for a small desk and a huge man sitting behind it—a man so bald it was as if Rollison were looking at a wax head straight from a mould.

"Hallo, Mr. Rollison. Honour to meet you! Glad if I can help. Question of identifying some hair, I gather." He spoke with a kind of subdued boom, and although he used short sentences he strung them together as if there were no pauses in between. "I'm ready for you . . . Got some samples of Northern Italian Po Valley locks right here." He opened a drawer and took out a tray, stretched out his hand for Rollison's samples, and then stuck a watchmaker's glass in his eye. He screwed up his nose and his lips and his mouth, and even his bald head became wrinkled. Suddenly he dropped the glass from his eye and caught it. Head, nose, mouth and eyes became smooth again. "Yes—same hair. I wouldn't stake my life on it, but I'd give it under oath as an expert opinion."

"Well, well," said Rollison. "Did you have much of it?"

"A few pounds, that's all."

"Can you tell me who bought any from you?"

"Could do, if I had to," said Cottrell, "but I don't think I need to. I can put two and two together as well as anyone. Like to look down the list of my employees about the time I bought that hair?"

Rollison said: "Please."

"Got it ready." Cottrell was rather like a satisfied, slightly smug schoolboy. He opened a file on his desk and handed it to Rollison, then grinned, as if he knew what to expect.

There were twenty-one names.

One of them was Ethel Franken—the daughter of the Frankens who had been hanged.

"Thought that would shake you," Cottrell said in his soft boom. "Bound to, wasn't it? Don't ask me where she is now. She worked here up to the time of the trial, then went off. She was very good at her job. Wig-making, chiefly. Matched hair better than most people. Used to take work home. Anything more I can do for you, Mr. Rollison?"

Rollison looked down at the list.

"Yes," he said.

"Ask away."

"There's a D. Lee on this list."

"Oh, that's Daffodil," said Cottrell, "Dear old Daffodil Lee."

"Old?" Rollison almost barked.

"Just a figure of speech."

"Was she a friend of Ethel Franken?"

"Bosom."

"What?"

"Bosom friend—*close* friend. Friend of the family, Daffodil was. There was some talk about her marrying into it, as a matter of fact. Then all the murder business cropped up, and that was that. Don't tell me you know Daffodil."

"Slightly," said Rollison.

"Isn't she the greatest?"

"The greatest what?"

"Stop fooling me," said Cottrell, now booming in a kind of laugh which wouldn't stop. "Daffodil was like a load of sunshine. Happiest kid I've ever known. Funny in some ways, mind you—a naturist, as a matter of fact, didn't believe in foundation garments except those needed to keep the necessary up. Gosh, what a figure that girl has! How is she?"

"In a state of near melancholy," Rollison answered.

Cottrell stared, his boom fading.

"I don't believe it."

"It's quite true."

"Then something must have changed her," said the bald-headed man. "She was the happiest girl in the world."

Rollison left the Knightsbridge *salon* and walked thoughtfully along Brompton Road for ten minutes, then turned into the tube station, which was fairly empty, and went to a telephone kiosk. He dialled Whitehall 1212 and asked for Grice. Instead of Grice, a man with a frail voice answered.

"Hold on, Mr. Rollison," he said.

that! I made a note somewhere, now where did I put it?" Wrightson began a frantic search through his pockets as Rollison moved to the desk, lifted the telephone, and picked up a scrap of paper.

"Here it is," he said. "Jerry Bateson."

"*That's* the chap. You know, that commercial programme, *Late Extra*—rival to *Tonight*, if you know what I mean." Wrightson reached the Toff and pointed with a gnarled forefinger. "There you are, read what it says: 'Gotta be at the Studio in Lambeth at half-past five if you want to be on.' Didn't say nothing about a fee. Don't want to be on, do you?"

Rollison was staring down at the scrawled message as thoughts flashed through his mind. Jolly, the four girl artists and Catlin, were missing, and Daffodil, once in love with a Franken brother, as good as missing. He could not really be sure how the police would react next.

"Now wake up, Mr. Ar. This ain't like you."

"Do you know what, Percy?"

"What?"

"I'm going to be at that studio, but don't let anybody know, unless Jolly telephones or comes back. Make absolutely sure of it."

"Sure, Mr. Ar!"

"And Percy—telephone Ebbutt at the Exhibition. Ask him and all the others working days to be here at the flat this evening by seven o'clock. All of them except the men on nights. That clear?"

"Clear as mud, don't you worry! Something's going on in that crafty mind of yours. No, don't tell me." Wrightson's voice rose as if in surprise when Rollison moved towards the door. "Not going already, are you? Stay for a cuppa tea, anyhow."

"Not this time. One other thing," Rollison said.

"Shoot."

"If anyone calls—Grice, Fox, the press, Catlin, the Tussauds, anyone except Jolly, say you're as worried as hell because I didn't come back. Let them think that I'm missing, too."

A slow smile began to curve Wrightson's lips.

"You cunning old basket," he said. "Okay, Mr. Ar. Better go and see it through then, hadn't you?" As Rollison turned towards the kitchen quarters, the smile became seraphic. Then suddenly he exclaimed: "Hey! Mr. Ar."

It seemed to Rollison that he was filled suddenly with great alarm.

"What is it?"

"Tune the telly into the right channel for the *Late Extra* programme for me. I don't want to miss you when you come on," said Wrightson anxiously. "Star performer you'll be."

Rollison went first to Conning Square, and this time made no bones about picking the lock. He took away one each of the small heads of the girls, packing them with great care in a case which he lined with two pillowcases. Then he made for the newly opened Commercial Television Studios across the river at Lambeth. His welcome was warm and spontaneous.

"Good evening, Mr. Rollison."

"Good evening, sir."

"Mr. Bateson won't keep you a moment."

"Hallo, sir."

A dozen people appeared from divers passages and doorways, to have a glimpse of the Toff. Most peeped for a moment, and ducked out of sight. A lad in his late teens came up with an open autograph book and a half-bold, half-nervous smile.

"Would you be good enough to sign this, sir?"

Rollison said: "Of course," and sketched the symbol which Liz Bonham had been painting, added his initials and handed the book back to receive an "Oo, thanks." Two more came forward, emboldened, and then one of the tallest men Rollison had even seen came striding along a passage, hand outstretched, face so lined that it looked chiselled. It was a very familiar face.

"I'm Jerry Bateson, Mr. Rollison. I can't tell you how glad I am to see you."

"Now I know why we always see you sitting down."

"Just a little trick of the trade." Bateson led the way along corridors and up stairs and finally into a lounge with a mute television set in one corner, figures dancing on the screen, and a praiseworthy array of bottles. "What will you have, sir? . . . Nothing? . . . Sure . . . Afterwards, then. They're expecting us in the studio in five minutes or so, not for a real rehearsal, just voice levels and that kind of technicality." Bateson kept looking down at the big case, and went on, half-laughing, "Haven't brought one of the damaged heads with you, I suppose?"

"Still undamaged, I hope," said Rollison. "What I would like to do is . . ." he went on, in some detail, while Bateson listened, enthralled.

"Wonderful!" he exclaimed when Rollison had finished. "Now—it will need a quick bit of switching . . . Let's go and get it started." He stepped into the passage and almost cannoned into a bouncy looking middle-aged woman. "Maggie! The very girl I want. Nip along and tell Charlie we'll have the air-crash film on before the Toff, and we need the Toff at the table, not in the easy chair."

"But it's all set—" the 'girl' protested. She had a fine, mobile face.

"Unset it. This is the scoop of a lifetime—the Toff in action. Get a move on!"

Maggie, realising he was serious, turned and ran along the passage. Rollison and Bateson followed her, and saw big doors not far away, with a blue light above them, and words which read:

QUIET—REHEARSAL IN PROGRESS

Next to this was another sign in red but not alight, reading:

KEEP OUT WE'RE ALIVE

"This way," said Bateson.

The door opened onto a mock wall of some kind of fabric, above which lights shone brightly and shadows moved with a strange kind of furtive haste. A moment later Rollison passed the end of the fabric, and stepped into a world which seemed to be of make-believe. Huge cameras on silent-running wheels, great arc-lights like enormous eyes, microphones jutting out like impatient fishing rods, pieces of scenery and of stage sets, and four people moving from a contemporary-type desk while two technicians and Maggie took chairs away.

"Better get that case opened before we're on the air," Bateson said. "Let's go behind the screen." He lifted the case, placed it carefully behind the screen and pulled out the first pillowcase, then took out Liz's head. "My, she's something!"

One after the other the heads were placed on the desk, and photographs of Catlin and Jolly placed in front of them. Apart from the movement of cameras and men shifting the position of the lights, there was a hush over the studio. A microphone was pushed above Rollison's head and a young man in his shirt-sleeves came up, hopefully.

"Spare a moment, Mr. Rollison?"

"Yes, of course."

"Would you mind sitting—where do you want him, Jerry?—in that chair? Thanks." Rollison sat down. "Now say something. It doesn't matter what you say. What do you think of the latest James Bond film, for instance?"

"Never heard of James Bond," said Rollison promptly. Half-a-dozen people laughed, Rollison chuckled, and went on: "I can tell you what I think of the latest Beatle beat if that's what you want."

The bright young man, who had earphones clipped over his head, became momentarily distracted. Then he said as if to no one: "Okay? That's fine. Voice level's fine, Mr. Rollison. Now what about make-up? Maggie! Where the devil's Maggie?"

"Here," said Maggie in a sepulchral voice from just behind him.

"Oh, there you are, dear. Make-up. Bit of a shine on the forehead and we can't have the Toff on show with a shiny nose, can we?"

A raven-haired beauty in a bright pink smock put powder on Rollison's forehead, nose and cheeks, and said he looked lovely.

Something about the atmosphere had raised Rollison's spirits enormously, and he found it easy to laugh. Bateson took him by the arm, and whispered: "The show will be nearly on the air when we get back to the studio, so we'll have to be quiet. I'm going to interview you myself, but I won't say much unless you get stuck for words, and I don't think that's likely."

"How long do we have?" asked Rollison.

"Four minutes. We might squeeze four and a half."

"Try to," begged Rollison. "I feel I need half-an-hour."

"You'd bore the viewers over to the B.B.C.," said Bateson "Just cram in all you can. Don't worry about the camera but point to each of the little lovelies as you name them so that we don't show a blonde when you're talking about a brunette."

The red warning light was on when they reached the studio door, and they crept in. A nervous little woman was being interviewed by a man who kept asking her what had made her do whatever she had done.

"Well, I was so sorry for them, really, they were ever so hungry."

"She keeps seventeen cats," Bateson whispered in Rollison's ear. "We've got film of those. Over here—"

The four heads were in position, the photographs were on a stand ready for use, chairs behind the desk were empty.

"We're on after this."

A few minutes later a camera was wheeled in front of them.

"One of the most remarkable and intrepid men in London is the Honourable Richard Rollison, known to so many as the Toff," Bateson suddenly declared in a superbly casual way. "Mr. Rollison has been responsible for a startling number of successful investigations into crime, he is often consulted as an expert by Scotland Yard, and as a final accolade he is to be featured at Madame Tussaud's Waxwork Exhibition—only someone doesn't seem to want him there. Some person, or persons, unknown, has been trying to destroy wax models of his face—isn't that true, Mr. Rollison?"

Rollison smiled, slightly self-conscious with the camera fully onto him.

"Now if it were my face alone I could understand more easily."

"Do you know who's trying to stop you?"

"All I'm sure of is that it's a man or a woman who has been specialising in various disappearing tricks," said Rollison. "There are four most attractive young women—all artists—and two men who have disappeared while helping to find out who dislikes the idea of me being on show in wax. If anyone happens to have seen Miss Elizabeth Bonham about in the past twenty-four hours—" he pointed to Liz. "Or Isobel, a close friend of hers—" he pointed to Is. "Or—"

He could see the picture on a monitor set. Each model was shown in close-up; each was an excellent likeness. So were the photographs of Catlin and Jolly. When he had seen the photograph of Jolly, Bateson broke in as if unbelievingly:

"Do you mean that all *six* of these people are missing?"

"I mean that I can't find any of them, and I'm worried about them all," Rollison said. "There was another missing girl who was found yesterday, in a drugged coma, and a man I was most anxious to talk to was murdered only yesterday afternoon."

"Murdered!"

"That's the word."

"Can you prove it?"

"That's what the police asked me, too," answered Rollison drily. "And as they've arrested someone, presumably they believe me. No names, no pack drill and no libel or slander," he added. "But these disappearances have taken place since the trouble at Madame Tussaud's, and the people involved have all something to do with the case, so that means the police may soon want to ask some searching questions."

Bateson said faintly: "I'm sure they will. What do you want anyone to do if they've seen any of these people?" Close-ups of the heads and the photographs were being shown again in quick succession.

"Let me know," said Rollison. "Or let you know!"

A man on one side of Bateson was drawing a finger across his throat, which was puzzling until Bateson said, as if still in a daze:

"Well, thank you very much indeed, Mr. Rollison. We hope those girls are soon found."

A man on the other side of the studio began to speak into another microphone. He was with the foursome who had been moved hastily from the desk, and were now sitting in contemporary tubular steel chairs, all looking most uncomfortable. Someone answered. Rollison felt much warmer than when he had been talking. Bateson put one thumb up, and a forefinger against his lips. Then there was a pause, and Bateson relaxed and said:

"There's the commercial. Like to go?"

"May we?"

Bateson tiptoed towards the fabric wall, led the way towards the door, and out of it. He spoke as if he, not Rollison, had been the victim of the inquisitorial camera.

"How about that drink now?"

"Just the moment," said Rollison. "What's likely to happen next?"

"I shall get the sack," said Bateson.

Rollison was startled. "You're not serious."

"Half-serious. By now all the telephone lines we've got will be jammed with people who've seen those girls, or think they have. I didn't realise how vivid the show would be." He led the way into the room where Rollison had first entered. One elderly and one youngish man were already there, glasses in hand.

"Marvellous, Mr. Rollison!" one said warmly. "Couldn't have come across better."

"You'll probably hear that the girls have been seen from Land's End to John O'Groats," said the other. "But you were after something like that, of course. I wonder if—"

A telephone bell rang.

"They've started," the speaker said. He lifted the telephone. "Guest Lounge . . . Yes, he's here. For you, sir." He handed the instrument to Rollison.

"What will you have to drink?" whispered Bateson.

"Whisky and soda . . . Hallo, Richard Rollison here."

"Mr. Rollison," a man said in a hoarse whisper. "I know where all those people are. Don't make any mistake, I really know. How much is it worth for the information?"

Rollison did not answer immediately. He was aware of Bateson pushing a glass towards him, staring all the time, but that seemed vague and unimportant. He saw the mute images on the monitor screen again. He seemed to hear the hoarse voice, repeating the words over and over again, until the speaker said anxiously:

"Are you there?"

"Yes, I'm here."

"Well, how much is it worth?"

"How much do you want?"

"I'm not cheap, Mister." There was a long pause. "Say five hundred quid."

"Be at my flat in half-an-hour."

"What do you take me for?" interrupted the speaker. "Photographers and newspaper-men are littering the doorstep, and the police too, I wouldn't wonder. If you want to know where they are you've got to come to me."

"Where?" asked Rollison.

"How about the entrance of the Ritz-Hilton, Kensington, at eight o'clock. I'll see you there."

The man rang off.

Rollison sipped his drink, aware how intently the others were all looking at him. It would be easy to tell the simple truth, that he felt quite sure that the message was another hoax, that it would be dangerous to do what the caller asked. In fact he was so surprised by the quickness of the response that he did not know what to say for the best. Before he could make up his mind the telephone bell rang again.

Bateson picked up the receiver.

"Is that for Mr. Rollison? . . . Just take messages, and be as polite as you can about it. Tell them that Mr. Rollison will be in touch as soon as he can." Bateson put down the receiver. "You've got to have a breather, damn it."

"Yes," said Rollison. "Thanks. I didn't expect a response as quickly as that. Have you anyone who can take messages?"

"We could rustle someone up."

"Will you, please?" asked Rollison. "I'll get in touch with my flat. That first call might be the one I'm after," he added, then swallowed his drink. "Do you think you could get me a taxi?—and have these heads and photographs sent on to me in another one?"

"Of course," Bateson said. "So you think it got results?"

"We'll know for sure before long," Rollison said.

Five minutes later, he stepped out of the television building towards a waiting taxi. As he did so, a car pulled up in front of the cab, and a door opened and Superintendent William Grice stepped out.

CHAPTER 15

THE MAN WITH THE HOARSE VOICE

"You won't need the taxi," said Grice.

"I don't need a Black Maria, either," Rollison retorted.

"I'll drop you wherever you want to go."

"Did I hear someone say that that taxi's free?" asked a young man who came up with a fragile-looking young girl. "Oh, fine—thank you very much."

Rollison climbed in next to Grice, who was driving. No one else was in the car. Grice did not speak until he was moving off into a flow of traffic, when he said with a laugh in his voice:

"You get trickier every day."

"Would you have shown those girls?"

"We don't even know for sure that they're missing—at the earliest we would have shown their pictures tomorrow," Grice said. "But if you get any response I want to know at once."

"I daresay you do," Rollison said drily.

"Why didn't you report Jolly missing?"

"The Yard wouldn't yet admit that missing is the word."

Grice was driving skilfully through the traffic as Rollison answered. "What's mellowed you, Bill? From the way you froze me on the telephone and Fox used the high hand, I thought you'd turned your backs on me over this."

"Had to be careful," Grice said.

"How careful were you?"

"King's prints were on the knife with which Gant was killed. There's no doubt he did it, although when questioned at the Yard he said you did it. He's proved a liar in one way so we'll assume that he's lying and you're telling the truth." Grice sounded almost smug.

"And?"

"Do you want more?"

"Yes."

Grice said slowly: "Daffodil Lee has come round. She says she didn't know she'd been to your flat, and that whoever doped her it wasn't you. We rather thought you might have, to make sure she didn't tell us what she knew."

"Well, well," said Rollison. "Have you questioned her?"

"The doctor says we can ask her a few more questions after nine o'clock tonight, and not before."

"Where is she?"

"At the Maidens Nursing Home."

"May I be there when you question her?"

"If you want to be."

"That's better," Rollison said feelingly. "That's much better."

He could not make up his mind whether to tell Grice about the man with the hoarse voice. Grice obviously didn't suspect that he had already had a call. If Rollison told of the man, the police would almost certainly want to watch him until after they had met at the Ritz-Hilton, but the telephone caller might realise that the police were watching, and keep in the background. The urgent question was whether to take a chance on his own or not.

"Are you seriously worried about Jolly?" asked Grice.

"Yes."

"Why?"

"He wouldn't keep away without sending a message if he could avoid it."

"How do you know he hasn't sent a message?"

"If he had, Wrightson would have telephoned from the flat," answered Rollison. It was then that he made his decision, and yet when he went on it was a relaxed voice. "Drop me off at the flat, Bill, will you?"

"If you get genuine messages, remember I want to know."

"Bill," said Rollison, "if you care to send a couple of men round to the flat, they can man the telephone for me. There'll be dozens of messages—here, at the studio and probably at the Yard as well."

"I may take you up on that," Grice said, and added: "Rolly."

"Yes?"

"Has it struck you that you are very nearly the only man involved in this who isn't missing?"

"It's struck me very forcibly indeed," Rollison said. "Has King talked at all?"

"No."

"Is he legally represented?"

"He asked for legal assistance after he was remanded for a week this morning, and of course he'll get it."

"Have you found out much about him?"

"No," answered Grice. "That's one of the things which worries us most. He's given a hotel address, where he stayed for three nights. The home address he gave was fictitious. I've had his photograph sent out all over the country, but there's no report on him yet. No one knows why he killed Philip Gant, or whether they've been associated in the past. He's just appeared out of thin air."

"As the others have disappeared into it," said Rollison drily. "Have you tried the Frankens?"

"Do you mean if I've checked whether they know King?"

"Yes."

"No, I haven't."

"Did you know that Daffodil Lee was practically engaged to one of the Franken sons?"

Grice didn't answer.

"Did you?" insisted Rollison.

"No, I didn't," admitted Grice. "That's most peculiar. I thought I knew all of the friends and relatives of the Franken family. Are you sure of this?"

"Her ex-employer told me about it."

"Who's that?"

"Cottrell, the court hairdresser of Knightsbridge."

"I'll do some more checking," promised Grice.

He was moving in a stream of theatre traffic along Piccadilly, and turned left then left again into Gresham Terrace. A few men were gathered about the street door of his house, but few people were in the street. Both kerbs were packed tightly with cars. Grice drew up, and Rollison asked:

"Coming in for a drink?"

"I want to go straight over to the Yard."

"Then don't get out." Rollison jumped out, closed the car door, and neatly side-stepped three men who bore down on him almost as soon as the car had moved off. A flashlight went off, so bright that for a moment it nearly blinded him. A man called:

"Have they signed you up for a series after that performance, Mr. Rollison?"

"I shall get signed off if I don't start answering the telephone," Rollison retorted. "Make a path, will you? Unless anyone else wants a pretty picture."

There was a general chuckle, and they let him through. He hurried up the stairs, taking his key out as he reached the top flight. Had Jolly been home he would have been keeping watch, and by now the door would have been open. It wasn't. He inserted his key, turned and thrust the door back. As he did so, two men appeared on either side of the door—Ebbutt's men, obviously on guard. They relaxed as they recognised him, and one man called:

"Here's the Toff!"

Beyond the lounge hall, the big room seemed to be crowded with men all gathered about the television. Big Bill Ebbutt heaved himself out of Rollison's favourite armchair and strode towards him. Everyone else glanced round and there was a chorus of "Evenings," but most of them turned back to the screen at once.

"Bit o' boxing," Ebbutt explained. "Two of my lads are at Earls Court tonight—how about that, Mr. Ar—you *and* a couple of my lads on the same evening? That was a knockout show you put up, too. Congratulations."

Rollison said: "Thanks. How many messages, Bill?"

"Messages? What messages?"

"Hasn't anyone called about the missing girls?"

"Haven't had a single call since I arrived an hour ago," Ebbutt assured him. "Been ever so nice and quiet, Mr. Ar." As he stared at Rollison the significance of the telephone silence obviously dawned on him, for he drew in a wheezy breath, and exclaimed: "You ought to have had dozens of calls! I was so carried away I never gave that a thought."

"Let's see if the line's been cut outside," Rollison said.

The line had been cut near the back door, from which the flat was serviced. Calls could not be made to, or out, of the flat.

"They're pretty good," Ebbutt said, much more troubled than he had been. "Beginning to worry me, they are."

"Bill," Rollison said, "I'm going over to the Ritz-Hilton at Knightsbridge. It's on Park Square. I want you to have a man outside the main entrance and one at each side of the Square in half-an-hour from now. Don't do anything unless I give word, or unless I'm not out by ten o'clock. If I'm not, telephone the Yard. Will you do all that?"

After a pause, Ebbutt opened his mouth and let out a stentorian bellow.

"*Hey, there!*" Every head turned in unison. "Turn that flickering box off and listen to me . . ."

Rollison heard Ebbutt giving instructions as he himself went into his bedroom, opened the wardrobe door, went down on one knee and unlocked a drawer at the bottom. In here, he kept what it pleased him to call his 'box of tricks.' In fact there was an automatic pistol and ammunition, for which he had a licence. There were knives attached to bracelet-like clips which he could fasten round his arm or his leg, and there were some tiny glass phials of what looked like a cigarette lighter fuel, but was in fact tear gas which would vaporise on bursting. He put four of these into white cylinders which looked exactly like cigarettes, hesitated, and decided not to take the gun or knives. He was about to relock the drawer when he changed his mind, and clipped a knife about his left forearm. This did not affect his movements in any way.

Ebbutt was still giving orders.

Rollison went out the back way, watched the pale surface of the courtyard below, and then started down the iron fire-escape. Carefully though he went, there were faint metallic sounds, and once quite a loud boom. Whoever had cut the telephone wire must have made at least as much noise.

No one seemed to be about.

Rollison reached the bottom, slipped silently along an alleyway, and reached a street leading to Gresham Terrace in one direction and Piccadilly in the other. Soon he was in a taxi heading for the Ritz-Hilton. He looked through the rear window a dozen times, but no one appeared to be following him. He sat back, until the taxi pulled into the forecourt of the hotel. There were subdued lights, a dozen parked Rolls-Royces and Bentleys, three doormen and two pageboys. As he paid off his cab one of the doormen said:

"It's Mr. Rollison, isn't it?"

"Yes, that's right."

"Mr. Wax asked you to go straight up."

"Mr. Wax—" began Rollison, and then asked: "What room?"

"Suite 909, sir—on the top floor."

"Thanks." A boy opened the swing doors for Rollison, and stood smiling up. Rollison beckoned him as they went through.

"Do you know Mr. Wax?" he asked.

"I've seen him, sir."

"Has he been here long?"

"Only booked in today, sir."

"What is he like?"

Dark brown eyes were turned earnestly towards the Toff, the boy was obviously fighting with his curiosity, and then managed to conquer it.

"He's rather ordinary, I suppose."

"Like either of these people?" Rollison showed photographs of Jolly and Catlin.

"Oh *no,* sir."

"What did he speak like?"

The brown eyes were more puzzled than ever.

"Just like anyone, sir."

"Like me?"

"Well—not quite like you."

"Like the doorman?"

"No, not quite like him, either," the boy admitted. "As a matter of fact he sounded as if he had a cold."

"Ah," said Rollison. "Husky, was he?"

"That's the word, sir! Husky."

"Do you see him anywhere down here?"

"No, sir. But he's waiting for you upstairs."

"Well, well, of course he is." Rollison put two shillings into the boy's hand, and went thoughtfully into the huge foyer. A bookstall on the right was fairly busy. The porters' area seemed to be alive with men in pale grey uniforms, the clerks at the reception desk looked like models from *Men's Wear.* Rollison moved into the main lounge, which was walled with gilded mirrors. The high ceiling was supported by tall pillars which had small squares of glass on the surface.

Hundreds of people were in sight.

Rollison walked slowly round, making sure of two things: that Ebbutt's men had good time to get here, and that he knew no one in the lounge or foyer. Satisfied on both counts, he went to the main lifts. A girl who would have done credit to Henri, dressed in a puce-coloured uniform, took him up to the ninth and top floor.

"Suite 909 is to your right, sir."

"Thanks." Rollison turned right along a thick piled carpet which seemed to ooze luxury, past more mirrors and ornate lamp fittings and fine chairs and settees. He passed several doors, all pale grey, until he reached one which was marked 909.

A lot of things had passed through his mind in the past ten minutes, not least the fact that this palace of luxury seemed the last place from which any one of the Frankens would operate. It lifted the affairs into a financial level which in itself did not seem real—which seemed, in fact, like a hoax in itself.

There was a bell and a big brass knocker. Rollison pressed the bell, and just heard it ringing. It reminded him of the moment when he had rung the bell at the door of the girl's studio. It continued to remind him of that, because there was no answer. Each second seemed interminable. He rang again, with the same lack of response, so next he banged the knocker.

The door yielded. It did not open, but obviously it was not locked.

Rollison rang and knocked again, and the sound fell away into silence. He pushed the door and it opened enough for him to see inside. He glimpsed a beautifully furnished hallway in green and gilt, with nothing to suggest that anyone was in it. A medley of conflicting thoughts passed through his mind—that he might find another body, that he might find another damaged head, or a burnt-out eye, or even a photograph with a cigarette burn. He pushed wider, and saw four doors leading out of the hall, each of them closed.

There was no sound in front of or behind him.

He knew the risk only too well. Grice had let him get away with a technical forced entry once, but might not be able to again. Yet he was here, the trap was waiting, until he sprung it he could not hope to find out how deadly it might be. So he pushed the door wider open and stepped inside, sure that no one was behind the door, and no one was in this room.

He looked into the other rooms. Each was empty. What was more surprising, there was no indication anywhere that the suite was occupied, even the bathroom had an unused look, and a sani-seat was on the lavatory pan. Sure that every room and cupboard was empty, he went back to the passage; no one was near. At last he went to the final door, turned the handle, and pushed.

He darted back.

An effigy hung there, swinging gently where he had touched it—an effigy without clothes but with a head.

His head, with a rope round the neck.

CHAPTER 16

R.I.P.

ROLLISON felt the shock go through him as he stood watching the swaying effigy. The face was lifelike; it was like looking into a mirror. The hair looked natural—not by any means a wig, but inserted hair by hair, as by Eva at Madame Tussaud's.

Slowly, Rollison recovered his poise—but not his inward composure. He had expected something like this, and yet it came with a shock of surprise, and left him with a sick feeling that was of more than awareness of the danger. He had not needed telling that this campaign was aimed at breaking his nerve; although he had come prepared for shocks, the nature of the trick had affected him so much.

He moved forward, pushing the effigy to one side. What else would he find here? More heads of the girls, as he had at the flat? Or—a body? He pictured Philip Gant in the moment of his death, and all that had happened in the next few moments.

He had been a fool to go in ahead of Gant.

He had been a fool to come here.

He would be a greater fool to stay.

The silence was uncanny. He could imagine that hoarse voice, telling him that the speaker knew where the missing girls were.

Were they here?

He glanced round at the effigy, seeing it from behind for the first time. A card was stuck onto it, with three six-inch letters stark and clear:

R.I.P.

His heart hammered.

Whoever was doing this was very, very clever. The effect of the three letters was almost as great as that of the effigy. Unexpectedly, however, there was a secondary one, and he began to smile. Clever was the word: almost too clever. In a way it was like crying 'wolf' too often.

Rollison turned his back on the effigy and the R.I.P. sign, and studied the room. It was a bedroom with twin beds which were made and empty; there were no heads here. He crossed to the beds and made sure there were no more messages. When he went back to the hall, he hesitated. It was inconceivable that he had been lured here simply to see an effigy of himself hanging. He made a thorough search of each room again, and found nothing remarkable, nothing to cause any alarm. Satisfied, he went to the passage door. He took the handle, turned and pulled—and the door wouldn't open. He stared at it almost stupidly, and then began to smile again.

The door was locked, of course—that shouldn't surprise him. Nor did it shock so much. He pulled again, gently, with the same result. It had been locked from the outside, to make sure he couldn't get out.

A telephone bell rang in the front room. He went towards it, seeing the pale green instrument on a gilt table in the long window which overlooked a Square where dozens lazed in the evening warmth. He picked up the receiver.

"Richard Rollison," he announced.

"At least that is honest," said the man with the hoarse voice. "I am coming up to see you, before long."

"How long?" demanded Rollison.

"Don't be impatient—just wait for me," the man said. "Here is a little thought for your comfort. We've only just started on you. When we've finished with you, you'll wish you'd been hanged by the neck until you were dead."

He broke off, and the receiver went down sharply. Rollison replaced his, much more slowly, and there was tension in his smile. He moved away from the telephone, crossed to the door, and went down on one knee so as to look through the keyhole; he could just see light, so the key wasn't in the lock. He went to the big window overlooking the garden, remembering what it had looked like from outside. There was a small balcony, which led from the second bedroom, and it was close to the balcony of the bedroom in the adjoining apartment.

He could climb quite easily from one to another.

This was Apartment 909, so next door in that direction was 908. He lifted the telephone and asked for 908.

"One moment please," the operator said.

It was a long moment; in fact it was several moments. He looked down into the street and saw Ebbutt's man there, a short, broad ex-boxer, named Ford, who would stay on watch all night if needs be.

The operator came to life.

"I'm sorry, there's no answer from Apartment 908, sir."

"I'll try again later," Rollison said.

He went into the bedroom, past the effigy, and out onto the balcony. No one among the tiny creatures below was looking up. It was easy to climb on the rail of his balcony, and step across to the next. He dropped down, and stood back, trying to make sure that no one had seen him. He turned to the bedroom, exactly like the one he had left. The door was locked, but easy to force, and he stepped inside a room which was so redolent with perfume that he wondered if someone here had spilt a bottle.

Women's clothes littered the floor, the bed, the chairs. Powder spread like thick pink dust over the dressing-table and a chest of drawers. The wardrobe door was wide open, and expensive-looking dresses were crammed inside. Rollison took all this in as he went into the hall. This was tidy except for some letters, opened and dropped on the table, and a huge bowl of roses, at least three dozen of them, salmon pink and red and white and yellow. The scent of roses was almost overpowering, too. Rollison made sure no one was in the other rooms, which were just as untidy, then unlatched the passage door, pulled up a chair, sat down and prepared to wait.

"Don't be impatient," the husky-voiced man had said.

The greatest risk was that the occupants of this apartment would arrive before the man who had locked Rollison in. There would have to be a flurry of apology, and some quick manoeuvring.

He heard the faint whine of the lift. A man said: "To your left, sir." No one answered but a man came towards Rollison who stood close by the door, which was open only a crack; and Rollison peered through.

A man from Tussaud's, the cast-maker Wilberforce, passed the door. He stopped almost as soon as he was out of sight, and the sound of metal on metal followed. He opened the door of the next apartment, and Rollison heard him call:

"Well Rollison? Have you waited long enough?"

Rollison began to smile.

Wilberforce closed the door, and as he did so Rollison slipped out and put his head close to the door.

"Don't play the fool," Wilberforce called clearly. "And be careful I have a gun."

Rollison was smiling almost beatifically.

"Rollison!" Wilberforce called.

There were other sounds, obviously as he moved about the apartment Doors slammed. There were moments of silence, before another door slammed, and Wilberforce asked helplessly and angrily:

"Where the hell is he?"

Rollison stood to one side, only just in time. The door opened and Wilberforce strode out. His left hand was in his pocket, probably holding the gun he had boasted about. He did not see Rollison, who was flat against the wall, but pulled the door to and started for the lift.

"Going somewhere?" inquired Rollison.

As Wilberforce started, violently, and snatched his hand from his pocket, Rollison put out a leg and hooked his ankles. Wilberforce fell. Rollison did not break the fall. He saw the dull metal of an automatic slide out of the man's pocket, and kicked it away. Wilberforce banged his head on the wall, and appeared to be dazed, even semi-conscious. Rollison opened the door with his foot, bent down and gripped Wilberforce's ankles. He drew the man unceremoniously into the apartment, closed and bolted the door, then dragged his victim over the thick carpet into the bathroom. By the time they were there, Wilberforce's eyes were wide open and he was waving his arms about and gasping for breath.

Rollison moved the lever which controlled the plug, and turned on both hot and cold water at full pressure. The sound of roaring water was deafening. Wilberforce tried to say something but could not make himself heard. He tried to scramble to his feet but Rollison simply put his foot against the man's chest and pushed him flat on his back.

"What the hell are you doing?" screeched Wilberforce.

"Getting ready to drown you," answered Rollison.

"What did you say?"

"I'm getting ready to drown you."

"I can't hear you!"

"Can't you?"

"What?"

Rollison leaned forward, turned off the taps and said with great clarity:

"I am getting ready to drown you, Wilberforce."

"You're crazy!'

"Whether I'm legally responsible for my actions won't make any difference to you."

"You're lying!"

"The bath is nearly full," Rollison said. "All I have to do is dump you in and hold you under. Everything will be over in a few minutes."

Wilberforce gasped, and said: "You're not serious," as if he was beginning to believe this was a real threat.

"I'm very serious."

Wilberforce stared at him with fear in his dark blue eyes. He darted a glance towards the door, and Rollison moved across and closed it. Immediately Wilberforce looked at the ventilation grills.

"No one would hear the water gurgling through that," Rollison remarked.

"You are crazy!"

"No, just mad," Rollison said. "Mad with you for damaging the model you made, for burning holes in it, burning an eye out of a photograph, for laying on all this, including the R.I.P. It would be a pity to waste that card, wouldn't it?"

Wilberforce said gaspingly: "What—what—what can I do to—" he broke off, as if he really did not know what to say.

"You can try talk yourself out of it," said Rollison. "Just answer my questions. If I get the right answers, I might just douse you, not drown you. Where are the girls?"

Wilberforce gulped.

"Just answer," Rollison said. "Where are Norah, Is, Mandy and Liz?"

The man on the floor muttered: "I don't know. It's no use asking me, I don't know."

Rollison moved towards him slowly, menacingly. There was a look of mingled fear and defiance in Wilberforce's eyes. Rollison bent over him. Suddenly he struck at Rollison's face and kicked out at the same time. Rollison took the kick on his thigh, and gripped Wilberforce's wrists, pulling the man upwards. Wilberforce was gasping. Rollison hauled him to his feet, and pushed him towards the half-filled bath. Wilberforce began to struggle, but was helpless. Rollison forced him to sit on the edge of the beautiful rose-pink bath, then slowly pushed him backwards.

One thing was certain; Wilberforce could not be sure whether Rollison would push him under the water or not. He might argue with himself, might persuade himself that it was an empty threat, but he could not possibly be sure.

He opened his mouth.

"Mr. Rollison, don't do—"

Rollison kept the grip on his wrists with one hand and pushed him remorselessly backwards. The colour ran into Wilberforce's face, his eyes half-closed, his mouth went slack. Rollison kept pushing, but kept his free arm on the man's legs so that his whole body could not topple backwards. Mercilessly, he pushed until first the back, then the top of Wilberforce's head was under water.

Relentlessly, he pushed him right down.

The terror in the man's face was horrible to see. He closed his mouth to try to keep the water out, but knew it was too late. He drew in a great gulp of water, choked, tried to raise his head above the surface, but could not.

Rollison held him under for only a few seconds, and even in that time the man seemed to be losing consciousness. Once pulled up, Wilberforce began to retch. Rollison turned him round so that he was leaning over the bath. The only sound was the man's retching which quietened at last.

Rollison said: "Don't make any mistake. I will do it if you don't talk. Nod your head if you heard me."

Wilberforce nodded weakly, as water drooled out of his mouth.

"Answer each question with a nod. First—did you damage the cast and the photograph?"

Nod.

"Did you do it out of personal revenge?"

Shake.

"Did you do it for money?"

Nod.

"Was Daffodil involved in this?"

Nod.

"Did she pay you?"

Shake.

Rollison paused, and the only sound was Wilberforce's heavy breathing. Rollison placed a hand at the top of each arm and raised the man up, steadied, and guided him towards the W.C. seat. He sat him down on this, and drew back. Wilberforce, still breathing hard, looked up at him through his lashes.

"Do you realise that I mean what I say?" asked Rollison.

Wilberforce nodded.

"You've got a tongue in your head."

The other man gulped.

"Yes, I know you mean what you say."

"Now answer my questions. How was Daffodil Lee involved?"

"She—she hated you."

"Why?"

"You can't be as dumb as that," Wilberforce muttered.

"Just answer my questions. Why did she hate me?"

"Because of the Frankens."

"What was she to the Frankens?"

"She was engaged to Arthur Franken, but he wouldn't go through with the marriage after—after his parents had been hanged."

"Why wouldn't he?"

Wilberforce flashed: "Use your head!"

"I'll put yours under again if you don't answer."

Wilberforce muttered: "Arthur wouldn't let her become involved in a family of murderers. That's what he said. He's planning to leave the country and to change his name—but he won't take Daff."

"And that is supposed to be my fault?"

Wilberforce showed another flash of courage.

"Well, isn't it? You hounded the Frankens until you had two of them hanged and ruined the others."

"I helped prove they were murderers."

"You may believe they were but Daffodil doesn't."

"Did you know Daffodil before she joined Madame Tussaud's?"

"No."

"Why did she join the staff?"

"After they'd decided to put the Frankens on display— she'd always been interested, she's quite an artist, so she managed to get a job after a lot of trouble. Jobs aren't easy to get at Madame Tussaud's. You want to know why she was so keen?"

"Tell me."

"She meant to burn the place down if they put the Frankens on show. The one way she could do it was by being on the inside. Then when you were brought in—" Wilberforce broke off, sneering: "Even you can see how she felt."

"I can see how you want me to think she felt," Rollison said. There must be another explanation for Daffodil joining Madame Tussaud's, but there was no way of being sure that Wilberforce knew what it was. Rollison did not force that issue, but asked icily: "Where did you come in?" When Wilberforce did not answer, he went on roughly: "The water's still in the bath."

"You wouldn't drown me," Wilberforce said almost jeeringly. "But you might as well know, I lied about Daff paying me. She paid me five hundred pounds to help her."

"So she gave you five hundred pounds," echoed Rollison. Now he was quite sure Daffodil had some different reason for working at the Exhibition. "When was that?" he demanded.

"Soon after she joined Madame Tussaud's," Wilberforce answered. "If it was worth it to her, why should I care?"

"Perhaps you will care about this?" Rollison said. "She has been unconscious for over twenty-four hours. The police are watching at her bedside. She didn't send you here tonight. She didn't tell you to telephone me about this hotel. So who else is involved?"

After a long pause, Wilberforce answered:

"You want your t's crossed and your i's dotted, don't you? Jack Franken did, that's who. And I tell you another thing, Rollison. He won't rest until he's put you where his Ma and Pa are—*and* sent you the same way, too."

CHAPTER 17

NEWS VALUE

IT would be easy to push the man back in the water, or to strike him, or to threaten him. Rollison did none of these things. There were things he could almost admire about Wilberforce, although nothing in his expression indicated that. Moreover, this man had said the same thing as King, with rather more detail, and both pointed an accusing finger at Daffodil Lee. The sooner he could talk to Daffodil the sooner he would know the whole truth; he was quite sure he had not heard everything yet.

Abruptly, he asked: "How well do you know Kenneth King?"

Wilberforce answered: "Well enough."

"He's been remanded on a murder charge."

"Thanks for telling me what I know already."

"Why did he kill Philip Gant?"

"Who said he killed him?"

"I saw him."

"That only makes you a liar."

Rollison said very thoughtfully: "I wonder if you'll hang together. Where are the other four girls?"

"Resting."

"Where?"

"Ask Jack Franken—it's a waste of time asking me."

"I have a feeling it's a waste of time talking to you about anything," said Rollison. "But I'll have one more try. Go and see Franken and tell him I want those four girls back at their studio by ten o'clock tomorrow morning, not only alive but conscious, not only conscious but well."

Wilberforce stared as if he could not believe his ears.

"And tell Franken that I'll put him where his parents are, and in the same way, unless he does what I tell him," added Rollison.

He turned and went out, without looking back. He carried a mental picture of a bedraggled Wilberforce gasping at him as he walked across the apartment and then into the passage. As he went past the apartment next door he heard beat music, and fancied that he heard a girl singing. He went down in the life, and as he stepped out of the main entrance it was ten minutes to ten. Almost the first man he saw was Bill Ebbutt, talking to the man on duty opposite the front entrance.

"Just checking up on you," Ebbutt said. "Seeing as how it was nearly ten o'clock. Any luck?"

"Do you know a man named Wilberforce at Madame Tussaud's?"

"Know him by sight, Mr. Ar."

"He'll be coming out soon," said Rollison. "Spread the word to all of your chaps that I want to know where he goes. I should think it will be ten minutes before he shows up."

"I'll see to him," promised Ebbutt, with complete confidence. "Don't you fret. Mr. Ar—"

"Yes, Bill?"

"Any need to worry about Jolly?"

"I'm hoping not," Rollison said grimly.

"Not sure though? If anything happens to Jolly," went on Ebbutt, "I'll personally break his killer's neck."

A shiver ran through Rollison from head to foot. "If anything happens to Jolly," Ebbutt's voice still seemed to be saying over and over again, "I'll personally break his killer's neck."

Ebbutt could not have made his own fears more vivid. Jolly was still missing, and there was no possible doubt that he was in danger. That was a fact which Rollison had been refusing to face for hours, but it had to be faced in all its ominous meaning. The girls, even Daffodil, Catlin, the whole of Madame Tussaud's were as nothing compared with Jolly's safety.

The stakes could not be higher.

"Mr. Ar," said Ebbutt.

"Yes, Bill?"

"You know what you're up to, don't you?"

"I hope so," Rollison said. "How I hope so. Make sure that you don't lose Wilberforce. If I go after him, he'll recognise me. Have him followed, and then have the place cordoned off. I'll be at the flat."

"Don't you fret," Ebbutt said again. "We'll run him into his hole and keep him there."

Rollison turned into Gresham Terrace just after ten o'clock—and then almost turned back. At first, it was like a nightmare. Dozens of people were crowded about his front door, cars were double-parked halfway along the road, two policemen were trying to move the crowd along. Five men stood on top of two vans, one of them with a ciné-camera placed on top of it. The people were calling out, jostling with one another, and several waved copies of an evening newspaper. The window of Rollison's flat was tightly closed and no crack of light showed.

In a way this was the biggest surprise of the affair.

Near the fringe of the crowd was burly Charlie Lloyd, one of Ebbutt's men, looking dejectedly along the street.

A police car turned the corner close by Rollison, who whispered into Lloyd's ear.

"What's on, Charlie?"

Lloyd jumped on the half-turn. He had a broad, broken nose and little buried eyes, and one large cauliflower ear. His voice was unexpectedly melodic, with a trace of the Welsh which he had not spoken since his childhood.

"Why you scared me, Mr. Ar!"

"Shsh. What's happening?"

"These people all want to see you."

"See *me?*" The truth was dawning on Rollison.

"They say they've seen these girls, Mr. Ar—I beg your pardon, sir. They saw you on television, and they all want to help."

"Charlie," Rollison said. "Lend me your cap and coat, will you?"

"It will be a pleasure." Lloyd immediately took off his tweed jacket and Rollison slid out of his and donned Lloyd's, which was too big for him; it felt very heavy in the humid evening. Rollison took the other's cap and placed it lightly on his head, pulled it over his eyes, and went forward. Everybody was so busy pressing towards Number 22 that no one noticed those behind. Rollison began to push his way through. Now he could hear what people were saying.

"I'm sure I saw them—two of them together there were."

"I saw the dark one over at Battersea Park. Couldn't mistake her."

"You couldn't have, I saw her at Swiss Cottage."

"Three of them, I saw."

"Tried to telephone the T.V. station, but they were engaged."

"Wouldn't have come if I'd known how many would be here."

Rollison pushed through, as gently as he could. Reinforcements of police were now pushing the crowd to one side, and a loudspeaker shattered the night.

"Move along, please, don't stand there. Move along."

"If the owner of SLJ 350 doesn't move his car in two minutes it will be towed away. Other cars which will be towed away unless removed immediately are . . ." A stream of numbers was broadcast.

"Move along, *please.*"

People were more interested in the police than in Rollison as he fought his way towards the front entrance, where a policeman whom he knew well by sight was standing as if on guard. He did not recognise Rollison at first.

"No use coming in here—no one's allowed in."

"If you'll let me pass—" began Rollison.

"I said no one and I mean no one!"

"Even though I've a key?" Rollison tipped the cap from the back of his head. The policeman raised his eyebrows, and promptly stood aside. There was a roar from the top of the vans, a man shouted: "There he is!" and suddenly lights were switched on, blinding the policeman, shining on the back of Rollison's head. The cameras began to whirr, and at the same moment some of the crowd surged forward, calling out:

"Rollison!"

"Mr. Rollison."

"Hey, Toff."

"Toff! I've seen them!"

"Toff—"

"Just look this way for a moment," bellowed a camera-man in a tremendous voice. "This way, Toff."

Rollison turned, raised a hand, said out of the corner of his mouth: "Open the door," waved again, and stepped smartly backwards into the downstairs passage. A roar of disapproval came as the door closed with a bang, and then the noise was almost cut off. It seemed strange to be in the empty passage, making for the deserted stairs.

If any of his neighbours wanted to go out they were going to have a rough time. He went slowly upwards, taking off the heavy jacket. He half-expected to see news-papermen at the landing outside his door, but it too was empty. He heard no sound until he turned his key in the lock and pushed the door open.

"How the hell do I know if he's coming back tonight?" demanded Percy Wrightson of his wife.

"He would have told us if he wasn't."

"He could have been delayed."

"He's home and dry," Rollison called out, and almost at once Wrightson and his wife, who made two of her husband in width and probably four of him in weight, appeared at the door of the big room. "How are you two?"

"Never expected to see *you*, after that mob," Wrightson declared.

"What I want to know is, have you had supper, Mr. Rollison?" asked his wife.

"No—and come to think of it, I'm famished. Any messages, Percy?"

"Messages? After the workmen came and fixed the telephone, I counted up to forty-seven, and then I took the receiver off." Wrightson's manner made it clear that had been the only possible thing to do. "If you believe all you hear those girls have been seen all over England, *and* the north of Scotland, *and* the Channel Islands. Never known anything like it. Had to tell 'em to write to us, or else talk to the Yard or the television company. What else could I do, Mr. Ar?"

There was a risk that an important call would be held up, but if the line was blocked by incoming calls, that would happen anyway. Wrightson, now almost as lugubrious-looking as Jolly, was obviously afraid he had done the wrong thing.

"It it's really urgent, they'll catch up with me," Rollison said. "Pour me out a whisky-and-soda, Percy." Rollison moved to the Trophy Wall, and started at that broken shoe-lace. As he did so he remembered that Ebbutt's men were to get in touch with him if they ran Wilberforce to earth, so the telephone situation could be very dangerous indeed.

He took a glass from Wrightson's hand.

"Thanks, Percy." He drank. "Ah. Now—I've some bad news for you."

Wrightson said almost on the instant: "About *Jolly?*"

"No," said Rollison, and thought grimly: not yet. "I've asked Bill to call me. If he can't get through he'll tear a strip off you, won't he?"

After a long pause, Wrightson said airily: "Can't have that now, can we? O.K., telephone station." He put the receiver on the cradle, and immediately the bell rang. "See," he said in sour vindication, and lifted it again. "Allo . . . You 'ave, 'ave you? If you'll telephone White-hall 1212 or send a postcard." He rang off, and immediately the bell almost made Rollison jump. "'Allo? . . . Where . . . Ta. Now if you'll telephone Scotland Yard or send a postcard . . ."

By half-past eleven, Rollison felt as if he were in the middle of a fantastic nightmare. The phone was not quiet for five consecutive seconds unless Wrightson was speaking into it.

Then suddenly, Wrightson's tone of resignation changed. "Willie? . . . Why didn't you say so? 'Ang on. It's Willie Smith," he confided. "Says he's run your man down."

Rollison's heart leapt as he took the receiver.

"Willie?"

"I traced Wilberforce all right, Mr. Ar. In fact three of us did. We're watching the place right now, one at the back and one at the front, and me. I'm in that telephone kiosk at the corner of Quinn Street, Mr. Ar. Get me?"

Quinn Street, Fulham, was the street where the Frankens lived—and where Ebbutt's men had often stood on watch after the discovery of a broken shoe-lace. He did not say "are you sure?"—he was quite positive that there could be no mistake in these circumstances.

"Was anyone else at home?" he asked.

"Let himself in with a key," answered Smith. "But Jack Franken—you know, the big one—he's gone in since, and I've seen Ethel Franken in the front room upstairs. Still doesn't take the trouble to draw the blind right down." Smith almost managed to make a smirk vocal. "Any orders, Mr. Rollison?"

"Make sure no one leaves until I arrive," said Rollison.

The vans and the cameras, the cars and most of the people had gone when Rollison went down to the street, as if everyone realised that they were only wasting their time. The policeman was still on duty and several newspaper-men were there, too. As Rollison closed the door, one called out:

"Any news of the missing persons, Rollison?"

"Where are you off to?"

"Scotland Yard," Rollison answered, as if truthfully, and he looked at the men at the wheel of the police car. "Any hope of a lift?"

"If you like, sir."

"Thanks," said Rollison. No one followed, everyone seemed satisfied that he was in fact going to Scotland Yard, and that gave him some breathing space. As the car slowed down at the Piccadilly Circus traffic lights, Rollison said apologetically: "In fact I don't think I dare go to the Yard, I've probably jammed all the lines to 999 and Whitehall 1212. May I get out here?"

The driver was surprised into a laugh.

"Thanks," said Rollison warmly. "I'll do the same for you one day."

He was out of the car before the traffic lights turned green, and got into a taxi not far behind. He gave the Frankens' address, and then sat back.

Twenty minutes later, he was getting out of the taxi at Quinn Street in the Hurlingham part of Fulham, beside the Thames. It was a quiet residential neighbourhood, well-lit, with many cars parked outside the terraced houses, for there were few garages near. Willie Smith came across the road, and spoke as the taxi drove off.

"They're still inside, Mr. Ar."

"Thanks. Tell Bill's other men I'm going in. They're to start making inquiries if I'm gone more than half-an-hour."

"Right, Mr. Ar."

Rollison rang the bell. As he did so, he seemed to see his own effigy, hanging and swaying, and the words R.I.P. in bold black lettering. What would he find here? He waited only for a few seconds before a man's footsteps sounded. He wondered which of the two Franken brothers this would be. Handsome, decisive, bitter Jack? Or plain and homely, often befuddled and confused Arthur?

It was Jack.

He stared as if at first he did not recognise his caller. Then his expression changed in such a way that Rollison could hardly believe that his surprise was pretended. Jack moved back, a hand still at the door, and drew a deep breath.

"You've got the nerve to come *here?*"

Rollison put his foot in the door as the other man started to slam it. The door rebounded, almost hitting Franken in the face. Rollison stepped much closer.

"You'll talk to me or you'll talk to the police. Which is it to be?"

"You damned coward! Always hiding behind the police. Why, if I had my way, I'd—"

He broke off.

"Hang me, I know," Rollison said. "Wilberforce told me."

Jack Franken stared, and then echoed: "Who?"

"Wilberforce."

"Who's Wilberforce when he's at home?"

"I'm more interested in who he is when he's here," Rollison said. "I want to talk to him."

"There's no one here named Wilberforce," declared

Jack Franken. "There's no one here except the family, and the others won't want to see you any more than I do. Why, of all the nerve——"

"Save your breath," said Rollison curtly. "I want to see Wilberforce."

"I don't know anyone named Wilberforce!"

"Three men saw him come in here about an hour ago," said Rollison. "Stop wasting time."

As he spoke, he had a strange feeling of disquiet, almost of alarm. It was nonsense, of course, and couldn't be true, but he began to feel that the man in front of him did not know that Wilberforce had come here.

A woman called from along the passage.

"Who is it, Jack?"

"It's Rollison," called Franken clearly, and a new expression seemed to grow into his eyes. "He come here to try to pin something else on us, Ethel. Come and try to make him believe that the three of us are here on our own, and don't want to see him."

CHAPTER 18

THE FRANKENS

As Jack Franken spoke, another door opened at the head of the stairs, and a second man appeared. This was Arthur Franken. Jack, Ethel and Arthur, the children of parents found guilty of murder, and hanged by the neck until they had died. It was over a year since Rollison had stood on the threshold of this house. Jack had opened the door, then, appearing both surprised and a little excited by the identity of the caller.

"Dad, here's Mr. Rollison—you know, the Toff."

Mild-mannered Charles Adam Franken had come forward, hand at his *pince nez*. His meek little wife had seemed timid at that first meeing, but not really frightened.

All three Frankens who now stared at Rollison must be remembering, much as Rollison was. They must be feeling bitter, too.

Bitter? All the evidence was that they were feeling vengeful, that nothing short of Rollison's death would satisfy their lust for vengeance.

Ethel came along the passage, slowly. Arthur began to descend, one tread at a time. A car passed, behind Rollison, with a harsh engine noise. Rollison stood very still, until all three were grouped in front of him, Jack in the middle, the others at one side and a foot or two behind. They were quite nice-looking in their way; wholesome-looking, too. The girl was fair-haired and pretty in a doll-like kind of way.

"Why don't you go away?" she asked. "Don't you realise that we hate the sight of you?"

"I want to see Wilberforce," Rollison said.

"Wilberforce?" echoed the girl, as if puzzled.

"Wilberforce? Who's he?" asked Arthur.

"I told you, we don't know anyone named Wilberforce."

"Then let's settle for the man who came in about an hour ago, and hasn't left."

The three glanced at one another. It was easy to believe that they were genuinely puzzled. Of course, they might be putting on a very good act, a pretence of innocence, and yet nothing about their attitude seemed overdone.

"No one came here," said Ethel.

"We've been alone all the evening," declared Arthur.

"That's what I told him," said Jack, almost sneering.

It was impossible to disbelieve Ebbutt's man. There could be no doubt that Wilberforce had come into this house. Was it conceivable that the Frankens did not know about that?

Rollison said: "Do you mind if I look around?"

"You bet we mind," Jack answered.

"That's a pity," Rollison said. "I didn't want to bring the police here again."

"Police!" That was Ethel, shaken.

"Listen, Rollison—" began Arthur.

"A self-confessed criminal and accessory to murder was seen to enter this house by this front door, and hasn't been seen to leave by any window or any other door," Rollison told them. This wasn't the time to tell the Frankens what Wilberforce had said about them, so he went on: "I don't want to cause trouble for the sake of it. If you don't know the man is here, then you need to find him as much as I do. He certainly came in."

Were these three play-acting? Was their attitude part of a grand hoax? The way they reacted now seemed wholly genuine, and but for what he knew Rollison would almost certainly have been convinced.

"He'd better come in," Ethel said slowly. "That's the only way to convince him that no one is here."

Slowly, reluctantly, all three Frankens drew back.

"You know where to go," Arthur said bitterly. "You won't need us to show you around."

"The place is a mess," Ethel told Rollison. "We're leaving for South Africa the day after tomorrow. There's hardly a neighbour in the street who will look at us, let alone speak to us."

"Just tell us if you find anybody," mocked Jack.

Rollison felt on edge and very alert as he began to look round the house. There was something uncanny about moving from room to room and going back in his mind over the previous visits, when he had searched the place thoroughly for evidence against the Frankens. He would have felt better in a way had the others stayed with him, but they left him to his own resources. In every room cupboards were empty, tea chests and crates stood everywhere, partly filled with books and ornaments, oddments and china. Two spare rooms on the top floor were completely empty, and there was nothing to show that anyone had been up here for a long time.

In the bedrooms, wardrobes were empty, dressing-tables and chests were mostly empty too. So was every cupboard, every place where a man might be in hiding. Rollison looked under beds and behind curtains, on top of wardrobes and in every corner, but no one was here.

Every passing moment seemed to make this part of a fantastic hoax, in which Ebbutt's men had somehow been enlisted to help to fool the Toff.

He went to the living-room, where the trio were now sitting around a muted television set, the only piece of furniture in the room except the chairs and one table. They watched in silence as he examined cupboards and corners, then went into the kitchen and even out into the small back yard, to look in a coal shed and a toolbox.

They stared at the moving figures on the screen and ignored Rollison.

The only place left was the cellar; and in that very cellar Rollison had found that piece of broken shoe-lace. He opened the door to it, from the passage, and switched on the light. There was a faintly fusty odour, but no sound. He went slowly down the stone steps, not knowing what to expect, prepared for anything, and also for nothing at all. He reached the bottom. There were two rooms down here, one where old suitcases and oddments of furniture had been stored, the other had been almost empty.

The suitcases had gone, and the once-filled room was also empty.

Rollison went into the next.

A rubber balloon-type dummy hung from the grating of what had once been a coal-hole. His own face, the eyes blank and the lips slack, was turned towards him. A card exactly like the one which had been at the hotel was pinned to the effigy. R.I.P.

Rollison went towards it quickly, and examined the iron lid of the coal-hole. It was dusty and dirty but there were signs that it had recently been moved. Wilberforce had gone out this way, not through a window or a door, and Ebbutt's men had missed him.

The questions that had to be answered was: did the Frankens know?

"I tell you we didn't!" cried Ethel.

"I'd no idea anyone was here," declared Arthur.

"If you ask me, Rollison put it there himself," jeered Jack.

"He must have had a key," Ethel said breathlessly.

"We've nothing to do with that—that figure," Arthur stated.

"Probably someone removed the grating from the outside and lowered the dummy from the garden," suggested Jack. "Friends of yours, trying to involve us."

"This is awful," Ethel said with a catch in her voice. "Just as we were leaving."

"It's as if this house is accursed," Arthur said helplessly.

"It's as if we're cursed by Rollison," growled Jack. "Going to fetch the police, Rollison? Don't make any mistake, we didn't hang that thing there, but I wouldn't lose any sleep if it was you instead of a dummy. Who hates you enough to work on you this way, Rollison?"

Rollison said: "You three."

"We know nothing about it!" cried Ethel.

"Oh, ring the police and let's get it over," said Jack. "There isn't anything left for us. My God, how I hate your guts! If it hadn't been for you our parents would be alive, if it hadn't been for you Arthur and Daff would be married, we wouldn't have to move out of the house we've lived in all our lives. Go on, call the police! If someone doesn't get here soon, I'll strangle you with my bare hands. At least they would hang me for something."

There were tears in Ethel's eyes, and her voice was husky as she said:

"Don't talk like that, Jack. Please don't talk like that."

Rollison asked quietly: "When do you say you're going to move from here? The day after tomorrow?"

"Yes."

"Can I find you here tomorrow?"

"We'll be here," said Jack.

"I'll see you then," Rollison said. "In the meantime you might ask yourselves why Wilberforce, who worked at Madame Tussaud's, thought it worth saying that he was paid by you and Daffodil Lee to campaign against me, and why he used your house for an R.I.P. message."

"He's lying!" cried Ethel.

"If you believe that, you're a bigger fool than I thought you were," said Arthur. "If we wanted to do you any injury we wouldn't employ anyone else. And—"

"We wouldn't do anything," Ethel declared shrilly. "Don't you think we've suffered enough already?"

When he went out, Rollison checked the manhole, which was in the small front garden, protected by a high privet hedge. It would have been easy for Wilberforce to haul himself up through the manhole, replace the cover, and creep along by the hedge to the next garden—in fact two or three gardens away. The lamp-light was good enough to show Rollison where the grass had been trampled down, and all the signs were that this was the way Wilberforce had come. Similarly, it would have been quite easy for anyone to have blown the dummy up in the cellar; only a small inflator was needed.

The important questions wasn't how it had been done, but whether the Frankens had known about it.

The second most important question was whether Ebbutt's men should continue to watch the house.

"Bill's got it all sewn up," Smith assured him. "I'm on till one o'clock, got a relief coming, and he'll be off at six when another relief takes over. Don't you worry, Mr. Ar. We're as good as any coppers."

Rollison actually chuckled.

He walked until he was on a bus route, and went on top while they went across the heart of a nearly deserted London, strange because there was so much light in the sky reflected from the neon signs, and yet such stillness everywhere. Over to the right was St. Paul's, still floodlit; not far ahead Nelson was still picked out in the beams of light from the Admiralty Arch. Wrapped in darkness beyond Regent Street and Oxford Street was Marylebone Road, and Madame Tussaud's. His bus passed within a few hundred yards of it, and Rollison got off, walked past the Exhibition entrance. Inside, only a few lights showed, and the wax figures of policemen on guard, a card saleswoman and a commissionaire seemed as if they were human.

In there were the usual night-watchmen, and the men made available by Ebbutt. As good as any coppers, he remembered. He went round to Allsop Place and the back entrance; a light glowed over the porch. He tried the door. As he did so, he heard a sound behind him, and swung round.

A policeman said gruffly: "What are you up to?"

"Hallo," said Rollison. "Nice to know you're on guard." He moved into the light. "They won't let me stay here in wax, so I thought I'd call in person."

The man, massive and middle-aged, was obviously suspicious.

"Very clever, I must say. Who——" he broke off as he peered closer to the Toff. "Why, it's Mr. Rollison!"

"Right in one," said Rollison. "Is all quiet?"

"Quiet as the grave, sir."

"When do you check with the night-watchmen inside?"

"Every hour on the hour, I've just come to have a word," the constable answered. "Should be someone——ah, here they are!" Keys rattled, the door opened, and two men appeared at the doorway, one of whom Rollison recognised as an Ebbutt man, the other a stranger. They looked at him curiously while speaking to the constable. Everything was quiet inside, no trouble at all. Did Mr. Rollison want anything? They had been told to allow him in and to do anything he asked of them.

"Yes, I'd like a look round," Rollison said. "Particularly in the modelling room." That was where Wilberforce worked. "No need to wait, constable, Good night."

"Good night, sir."

The nightwatchmen led the way inside. There was an eerie silence everywhere, only dim lights glowed. Catlin's office door was wide open, so were several other doors, and light from outside showed in. Their footsteps echoed, and seemed to re-echo time and time again. Rollison was taken along the big workshop. The lights about the mirror were out, and a single lamp burned high in the ceiling, giving a dim glow upon the wax heads and faces, the masks on the walls, the glossy wigs. In the smaller room where Eva worked a blue light made everything look weird.

"Everything's okay," Ebbutt's man whispered.

"Has Wilberforce been in here tonight?"

"No one's been here," the night-watchman answered. "There are six of us, that's all. Like to see the others? Two are in the Chamber of Horrors, and two in the Grand Hall."

"Let's meet them," Rollison said.

The semi-darkness, with the wax effigies of the famous and the infamous people of the past, created an eeriness which was hardly surprising. Everywhere seemed clammy cold. The silence seemed to be broken only by a kind of sighing, as if the figures were trying to draw breath. Nothing moved. When the two men from the Grand Hall met Rollison and his companions near the top of the main staircase, they spoke in whispers.

"Everything okay, Jim?" one man said.

"Careless lot of cleaners," a big, short-necked man remarked.

"Why's that?"

"People bring their picnics with them and leave the stuff all over the place. Ham sandwiches, how about that? Couple of Coca-Cola bottles, one or two milk bottles—should have taken 'em all downstairs."

"Careless?" echoed Rollison's companion. "Lazy lot of so-and-so's, if you ask me, but I'm not interested in rubbish, Jim. We've got to watch out for fire. Any signs of anything?"

"Not a glimmer. Hope to heaven there won't be, neither. A fire in this place would just about—"

"Be able to see your way about, anyhow," Ebbutt's man said. "Okay, how about the Chamber of Horrors?"

"You're welcome," Jim said as if he meant it.

Rollison and his two companions went down the stairs and into the Chamber, with the dark alcoves and the figures and tableaux, all glowing like ghosts. Two other men, one carrying a torch, moved towards them. They spoke in whispers, too.

"Everything okay?"

"All okay."

"No smell of burning?"

"No smell of fire."

"Anything suspicious?"

"Everything's normal."

They walked past the effigies of murderers appearing faintly out of the gloom. There were Neil Cream and Patrick Mahon, Bywaters and Mrs. Thompson, Rouse and Palmer. The figure of Jean Paul Marat, sitting in his bath, was grisly even compared with the death masks of Louis XVI of France and Marie Antoinette. They went on, past the dim figures of Charlie Peace and Dr. Crippen, Landru and Caryl Chessman. Just beyond the American were the statues of the Frankens, and the place where the Toff was to be.

One of the watchmen caught his breath.

"Look!" he gasped.

One of Ebbutt's men cried: "Their heads've gone!"

There were no heads where there should have been two.

The heavy breathing of the men hissed and whined through the Chamber and it seemed to Rollison as if a clammy hand clasped his arm. He moved forward before the others, shining a thin pencil torch onto the empty spot.

The statues stood there, still as death—headless, or so it seemed. Rollison drew close enough to see that the wax heads had been melted and the beeswax had dripped down over the shoulders of the figures. The hairs which had been so laboriously inserted, lay over the shapeless mess like canopies.

The nightwatchman said in a scared voice:

"They were all right an hour ago. I swear it."

"I saw them, too," confirmed Ebbutt's man.

"Let's get the police," said the nightwatchman.

"Before we get anyone else I'm going to call Mr. Bernard," said Rollison. "Wait here, will you?"

He walked off, footsteps echoing like thunder. None of the men near the beheaded statues moved except Rollison. As he walked, he shone his torch onto the molten wax, looking for something to explain the melting.

Bernard Tussaud soon arrived, and helped in the search, but no other damage had been done, and there was no sign of fire.

CHAPTER 19

ASSAULT AND BATTERY

ROLLISON woke to a bright morning, Percy Wrightson standing by his side with the newspapers, and the tea tray on the bedside table. A radio was on in the flat, most unusual at this hour, making Jolly's absence even more noticeable. Wrightson had slept off his lugubrious mood, and spoke as Rollison struggled up to a sitting position.

"Everyone's favourite teevee personality, that's what you'll be. Top of the pops, don't you worry. Know what you did last night? Jammed Scotland Yard *and* the teevee telephones, no one could get a word in edgeways. Proper lark it was, but I wouldn't like to be in your shoes when the cops come round. Old Gricey's been on the blower twice already. I told him you couldn't burn the candle at both ends, you weren't in until after three, so it'll be ten or so before you wake up."

"What time is it now?" asked Rollison.

"Just after nine. Look at this one—taken outside last night. Ought to put you on a charge of causing a public obstruction, that's what." Wrightson grinned. "Or public nuisance, how about that? I—blast it, there's the front door bell."

He spread the newspapers in front of Rollison and went off.

Rollison sipped tea, glanced at the papers, all of which had at least one photograph of the scene last night, but none of which mentioned the damage at Madame Tussaud's. At the same time he cocked an ear towards the door.

He heard Grice's voice.

"Give him a chance, can't you?" Wrightson protested. "Ain't been awake five minutes, hardly got his eyes open."

Grice appeared in the doorway, immaculately dressed, his face set and not in greeting. He had two newspapers tucked beneath his arm. Rollison, holding a cup of tea, blinked up and said: "Another cup, Percy?"

"Not for me," said Grice.

"Never mind the cup," said Rollison.

"P'raps you'd like a glass of bitter lemon," Wrightson muttered, half under his breath. He went out, closing the door with a snap.

Rollison looked up at Grice, conscious of being unshaven, unwashed and only half-awake.

"I'm sure you didn't deserve that," he said. "Sit down, Bill."

Grice sat on the arm of a big chair.

"Apart from blocking both 999 and Whitehall 1212 for two and a half hours last night, causing a traffic block in and around Piccadilly for twice as long, and alerting half the nation about the missing people when you should have told us, you had an uneventful day," Grice said. "The Assistant Commissioner, the Commissioner and the Home Secretary all want me to put you in a cell before you do any more harm." Something in Grice's tone of voice and expression told Rollison that he himself did not feel so censorious.

"And before I've committed any crime," sighed Rollison. "What it is to live in a police state!"

"I want to know where you went after you left here."

"Bill," said Rollison. "I went to see a man who told me he knew where the missing girls are. He turned out to be one named Wilberforce."

"The model-maker at Madame Tussaud's."

"Yes."

"Did you know he was a friend of the Frankens?"

Rollison put his cup down.

"Are you sure?"

"Yes—an old family friend."

"No—I didn't know."

"At least you're prepared to admit something is new to you. Wilberforce was a kind of unofficial uncle to the younger Frankens, but he didn't use the name of Wilberforce."

"What name did he use?"

Grice said: "Lee."

Very slowly, Rollison put his cup down, and hitched himself farther up in bed.

"Daffodil?"

"Her father."

Rollison actually winced before he asked: "Has she come round?"

"Yes," Grice said. "And she's going to be questioned at half-past ten—in my office. I want you to be present."

"Ah," said Rollison. "There's a nasty ulterior motive to that, or you wouldn't let me get within a hundred miles. I'll be there."

"There'll be a car waiting outside for you," Grice said, and sounded positively grim.

Daffodil Lee looked like Spring. The period of enforced rest had certainly not harmed her. Her eyes were perhaps a little dreamy, and her movements rather slow, but her hair was beautiful and her skin was flawless, and her looks could hardly have been improved upon. She came into Grice's office, dressed in a light-weight, slinky, silky suit which seemed to mould her figure, and Rollison remembered his first impression, that she did not have much time for foundation garments. She was curiously like Marilyn Monroe at her sleepiest and most seductive. When she saw Rollison there was a change in her manner, and a glint drove the dreaminess out of her eyes.

"So you're here," she said.

"Hallo, Daff," said Rollison. "How's your father?"

"Why, you devil!" For a moment it looked as if she would throw herself at him. "Everyone you touch you—you—you contaminate! You devil!"

At last Rollison understood why Grice had wanted him here.

"How did I contaminate you?" Rollison asked.

"You didn't do me any good when you drugged me!"

"When I what?"

"Don't try to lie your way out of it," cried Daffodil. "You made me come to your flat and then you put a drug in a drink you gave me. You devil, devil, devil!"

"Yes, aren't I?" Rollison said softly.

"You can't deny it!"

"Oh, I deny it," Rollison said. "Who is Kenneth King?"

"I don't know anyone named King!"

"Daffodil Lee," said Rollison slowly, "your father called himself Wilberforce. He was a friend of Kenneth King. King took you to my flat. You were drugged when you arrived, and the only thing we don't know is whether you let yourself be drugged, or just let yourself be fooled."

"*You drugged me!*"

"Daffodil—"

"Don't let him talk to me, get him out of my sight!" cried Daffodil Lee. "He corrupts everyone who comes in contact with him. Look what he did to the Frankens, look what he did to Philip Gant. *He's* the murderer, he killed Philip!"

Daffodil broke off, as if she could not find the voice to

go on. She glared 'at Rollison, her eyes bright with tears of anger. Her fingers clenched and unclenched, her whole body was aquiver. When no one spoke she swung round on Grice, and gasped:

"Why don't you arrest *him* for Philip's murder? It wasn't anyone else, it wasn't—"

She broke off.

"Who wasn't it?" asked Rollison softly.

"It was you!"

"What is Kenneth King to you, Daffodil?" asked Rollison.

"I tell you I don't know 'anyone named King, I only know you're a devil, a devil, a devil!"

"You know him," Rollison said. "And you know where Jolly and Catlin and the other girls are. Where are they, Daffodil?"

"I don't know anything about them."

"You know."

Quite suddenly, she sprang to her feet and leapt at Rollison, trying to scratch his face, clawing him on one cheek, kicking and screaming. Grice jumped to his feet, but before he rounded the desk Rollison closed with Daffodil, and held her very tightly, so that her arms draped over his shoulder, and she could not get freedom of movement to kick or to strike him. There was a voluptuous warmth in her soft body even then; even as she screamed at him he could feel what ecstasy this woman could give a man.

"Let me go!" she screeched, and suddenly she snapped at his ear. He felt her teeth, felt a streak of pain, and almost let her go. Then Grice took her right arm and forced it upwards behind her, so that she could only stand and glare at Rollison, hatred livid in her eyes.

The door opened and two startled men appeared.

"What's up?" one asked.

"Need any help?" demanded the other.

"Send a woman officer," said Grice, "and get this woman back to the nursing home." He tried to make Daffodil talk when she had quietened down, but she wouldn't speak. She quietened down until she was almost placid, and allowed the policewoman to lead her out. At the nursing home, the policewoman stepped ahead of Daffodil, on the porch, and Daffodil pushed her violently in the back, then kicked her in the ribs, jumped over her, and ran into the street. One policeman tried to catch her, but she sped past him, and although he blew his whistle, she got clear away.

Rollison and Grice were unaware of this for some time. After Daffodil had been taken out of Grice's office, Rollison kept 'a handkerchief at his ear, and the white linen had big crimson blotches, blood from the bite and the scratch.

"Come along and wash that," Grice said. He led the way to a washroom, where Rollison examined the teeth and nail marks in 'a mirror.

"So long as I don't get rabies." He bathed the bite and stuck on a plaster, dried the scratch and left it open. "I thought you told me she didn't accuse me of drugging her."

"She changed her story," answered Grice.

"How long has she been like that?"

"Since she woke this morning."

"Accusing me all the time?"

"Rolly," Grice said, "I think she hates the very sound of your name."

"Does she indeed," said Rollison softly.

"What does that remark mean?"

"I think she wants you and me and the whole wide world to think that she hates my guts," said Rollison. "But I don't believe hate comes into it. She's a cold-blooded bitch who knows exactly what she's doing, whether she's looking dewy-eyed, or flying into a rage, or sobbing her stone-made heart out. Bill—she was supposed to be unconscious when Philip Gant was murdered, but she knows he's dead."

Grice said: "Yes," gruffly. "And since she left your flat a policewoman has been with her all the time. She couldn't have heard of Gant's murder—"

"Unless she was conscious at intervals at the flat, and heard about it. Or unless she knew Gant was going to be killed."

Grice looked almost smug.

"The doctors say she was certainly drugged all the time, so she knew in advance."

"Beautiful, isn't she?" mused Rollison softly.

Grice said: "But why has she done all this? What's it all about? Why should she 'and her father work up this campaign against you and Madame Tussaud's? If it were the Frankens I could understand, but this girl—" Grice broke off, raising his hands hopelessly. "Do you know more than you've told me?"

Rollison said: "Not for certain."

"What does that mean?"

"That the whole business has been a hoax, if I'm anywhere near the mark," said Rollison. "That they made it look like a dead set against me, and also made it look as if they were working for the Frankens, but in fact I was simply the Aunt Sally, there to be shied at and to distract attention from the main cause. And the Frankens could be in the same position—the apparent instigators, the obvious ones to be suspected while the real villains were able to go along doing exactly what they wanted to do."

Slowly, dubiously, Grice said: "I can see why you say that, but why should they behave that way? What are they up to? Who *are* they?"

Rollison shrugged.

"I'd guess Daffodil Lee, her father, the man with the *aliases,* and Kenneth King. I don't pretend to know why, yet. Two things stand out a mile."

"Which particular two?"

"That Philip Gant knew the truth and that was why he was killed. And that the plans first began to misfire when King was caught red-handed. So we need to know what an alcoholic ex-suicide squad hero knew about Daffodil, whether he hounded her because he was in love with her or because of something he knew about her. Right?"

"You could be," Grice conceded.

"There's another thing we know," Rollison went on, "Madame Tussaud's is bang in the middle of it—Wilberforce-Lee and his daughter and Kenneth King were using the place for some criminal purpose, and suddenly needed to find an apparent reason for being there—to cover up the real one. Simple, isn't it?"

Grice said: "Simple," almost waspishly. "Rolly, why do you think Catlin and Jolly have disappeared?"

"As pawns in a campaign to blackmail me."

"And the four girls?"

"When I saw King plunge that knife into Philip Gant I knew we were dealing with the most cold-blooded killers imaginable. And they know me or a lot about me, too. They know what I was able to do in the Franken case. They wanted to stop me altogether, or they wanted to frighten me—that's why I said blackmail—and they chose the way of kidnapping those girls."

Grice rubbed the bridge of his nose.

"Or," he said.

"Or what?"

"Or the girls are working with Daffodil Lee, and hiding so as to fool you."

"It's conceivable, but only just," Rollison said. "I can accept one girl as lovely as Daffodil the Delilah, but not four. If they're involved, I think they've been fooled." After a pause, he went on: "Two things, Bill. What kind of result was there to my appeal about the girls last night?"

"So far, seven hundred and fifty letters and statements here, half as many at the television headquarters, and probably another five hundred at other police stations. They're being listed, and the first analysis should be ready by midday. What's the other thing?"

"Do you know what caused the melting of the two heads last night?"

"In each there was a small battery with a tiny element which generated enough heat to melt the beeswax down. It might have caused a fire, too, but the wax was probably too heavy for the element."

"When were the elements put in?"

"During the making of the heads."

"In other words by Wilberforce, *alias* Lee, Daffodil's father."

"That's right," Grice admitted. Suddenly he grinned. "I've talked to Bernard Tussaud, who is having every head by Wilberforce taken off and examined. The element appears to have been controlled by a switch just inside the actual dummy itself, and it was easy to switch on."

"Do we know where the small model heads were made?"

"No. Certainly not at the Conning Square studio, or at Madame Tussaud's workroom."

"I've a feeling we ought to have a closer look at that house in Conning Square," Rollison said. "Kenneth King was there once, and the old crone of a landlady was as awkward as she could be. Shall we go?"

Before Grice could answer, the telephone bell rang, and Grice heard of Daffodil Lee's escape.

"There's just a chance she's gone to Conning Square," Rollison said. "Let's go."

"You've no right coming and worrying an old lady like me," the woman at Conning Square complained. "I should never have allowed those young women to live here. I'm too broad-minded, that's my trouble." She complained even more bitterly when Grice insisted on going into each apartment, using her pass key. There was nothing in any of them to help the inquiry. "I told you it was a waste of time," the old woman grumbled.

"We haven't seen your rooms yet," said Grice.

Alarm flared up in the faded old eyes.

"My rooms are my own. I don't have to show you them. Interfering with a poor old woman, you ought to be ashamed of yourself." Her voice became more and more strident as they went down to the sub-basement where she lived.

There was an old scullery, and in the scullery an old-fashioned gas copper, half-filled with beeswax. On the shelves were models and casts of heads and hands, feet and faces. It was like a miniature workshop at Madame Tussaud's. The old woman's face was like parchment as she watched Grice and Rollison examine all these things.

Rollison heard her gasp as he opened another door. It led to a semi-basement bedroom, with single beds in opposite corners. Men's clothes hung on pegs in the walls, pin-up photographs covered one wall, a radiogram and a television set stood in one corner.

"Now we want to know why you lied to us about this," Grice said grimly. "No more lies, now."

"You won't get a word out of me—not a word," insisted the old crone shrilly. "If a mother can't try to help her own sons, what's the world coming to?"

Wilberforce, *alias* Lee, and Kenneth King, *alias* Lee, were brothers.

This old woman was Daffodil's grandmother.

Daffodil's grandmother swore time and time again, that she did not know anything that would help to find Wilberforce-Lee, Daffodil, the four girls, or Catlin, or Jolly. The only possible source of information seemed to be the Frankens.

CHAPTER 20

TRUE OR FALSE?

ROLLISON had never seen three more frightened people. The two Franken brothers and their sister were pale, tense and alarmed. Now and again as Grice questioned

them in his office, Jack would try to make a sneering remark, but his voice became more brittle until finally he
fell back on monosyllabic answers.

"Did you know that Daffodil Lee's father was known as
Wilberforce?"

No.

"Did you ever see Kenneth King, Daffodil's uncle?"

No.

"Have you seen any of these girls or these men?"

No.

"Did you pay Daffodil's father to damage the wax face
at Madame Tussaud's?"

No.

"Have you been to Madame Tussaud's in the past
month?"

No.

"Why did you break off your engagement to Daffodil
Lee?" That was directed to Arthur Franken.

"I knew what a hell of a life it would be in the future."

"Is that the only reason?"

"Isn't it enough?"

Rollison, standing unobtrusively by the window, interrupted for the first time since the trio had been brought
in.

"Did Daffodil do anything to make you change your
mind?"

Arthur glanced at him as he muttered: "No."

"Did you know Philip Gant?"

"No! I keep telling you—no, no, no!"

"Let me tell you something," Rollison said sharply.
"Even without the murder, conviction on the charges
would land you in prison for years. Do you realise that?"

"I tell you we haven't committed any crimes," Arthur
Franken said almost deperately. "I know you always
thought we helped our—our parents, but we knew nothing
about what they did."

Suddenly, silence fell—a shocked kind of silence. Never
before had any of the Franken children admitted their
parents guilt, but now it was out. Rollison asked almost
gently:

"Does that go for you, Ethel?"

Ethel looked as if she was about to burst into tears. A
glint of reflected sunlight made her fair hair look almost
like Daffodil's, and unlike Arthur, the bright daylight
made her look more, not less, attractive.

She nodded.

"Jack?" asked Rollison.

"Oh, have it your own way," Jack growled.

"Superintendent," Rollison said to Grice, "one thing was quite positive in your investigations into the murder, wasn't it? That the older Frankens had help."

Grice said quietly: "Unquestionably."

"And they refused to name their helpers, so we assumed they were protecting their children."

"I don't know what you assumed," said Grice. "I simply regarded it as one possibility."

"We knew nothing about it," Arthur insisted. He moistened his lips. "We often talked about it, at first we couldn't believe it had really happened. Then—then—"

"We lied to try to help them," Ethel said huskily.

"Who wouldn't, for their own parents?" demanded Jack.

"If you three didn't help them, someone did," said Rollison. "Daffodil was often at your home, wasn't she?"

"Yes," Arthur said.

"She knew the place well, she could have got hold of a key, and she could have served as a go-between where your parents and their accomplices were concerned." When none of the Frankens answered, Rollison went on in a harsher voice: "You began to suspect Daffodil Lee. Is that why you broke your engagement?" When there was still no reply, Rollison went on exasperatedly: "Haven't you got yourselves into enough trouble lying for other people? Did you begin to suspect Daffodil?"

Ethel actually began to cry, and put her hands in front of her face.

Jack said almost inaudibly: "It's no use, Arthur, he'll worm it out of you. Yes, Daffodil—Daffodil asked a lot of questions about—about diamonds which our cousin was supposed to have brought from Africa with him. He brought some in legally, and smuggled a lot more. She just hinted at it, kept on talking about it, said our parents surely hadn't killed the old chap for the inheritance only. Arthur—Arthur and Daff had a hell of a row, and broke off the engagement."

"Diamonds," breathed Rollison.

"Diamonds," said Grice. "Do you know to what value?"

"Daffodil said there was a handful of them," Jack answered. "We knew Ben had a diamond mine in West Africa and brought some to sell, but we never knew that he'd brought any in without paying duty. Daffodil seemed sure that he had."

"I told you before, they're lying. They asked me if *I* knew where the diamonds were," insisted Daffodil Lee.

"You're making it up," Kenneth King, *alias* Lee, said when Grice visited him at Brixton prison, where he was under remand. "I never knew anything about the murder, or any diamonds."

"Lies, lies, lies!" cried the old woman at Conning Square. "Nothing but lies, every word of it!"

Not long afterwards, Grice telephoned Rollison and said:

"A surprisingly large proportion of the reports after your television performance say those girls were seen near Baker Street and the Marylebone Road just before they disappeared."

"That shouldn't surprise us," Rollison said.

Early that evening, Rollison went into Madame Tussaud's. There was a queue half-a-mile long waiting to get in, and the entrance hall as well as all the galleries were choc-a-bloc with goggle-eyed people. A queue stood waiting outside the Chamber of Horrors.

"Jammed so tight in there, sardines aren't in it," said Bernard Tussaud. "We've never known it so full, even in the school holidays." They were in Catlin's office, away from the crowd.

"Good for business," Eva said brightly, but anxiety showed in her eyes. "Isn't there any news of Jim Catlin, Mr. Rollison?"

"Not yet." Rollison thought bleakly of Jolly. "Bernard, how easy would it be for some of the visitors to stay behind after the Exhibition's closed?"

"Easy enough if they really wanted to," said Bernard. "They often get left behind by accident. Some of the kids hide behind the statues, too, especially in the tableaux. Why, who—" he broke off, and then added in a strangled voice: "Do you think some of them do stay behind?"

"Last night the night-watchman found odd packets of food and some empty bottles," Rollison said. "It would be easy to dodge from one tableau to another, even to hide behind or beneath some of them. And these melted heads—"

"They could be looking for something buried in the wax of the heads," Bernard said thoughtfully. "We once had a worker who picked pockets and handbags. Guessing he was under suspicion he hid small articles in the wax he was using for heads and necks. When he thought it safe, he melted the heads down, but we caught him. Mr. Rollison, if you're right, the criminals used this place to hide in, and also to hide their victims in. Every single figure will have to be examined—my God, what a dreadful thought." He was as pale as any of the Frankens. "We'll have this place sewn up like a safe, tonight—no one must have a chance of staying behind."

"But we want them to stay behind," Rollison declared. *"What?"*

"If we drive them out we can't catch 'em red-handed, can we?"

Bernard moistened his lips.

"No. No, I see what you mean. What will you do?"

"First I'll talk to the police," Rollison said. "I think they'll want your chaps to behave exactly as they would normally—including Ebbutt's men—and prepare a surprise packet for later in the evening. The watchmen usually make rounds of all the halls, and then go off for an hour before starting the rounds, don't they?"

"That's right, Mr. Rollison. I can easily believe that some of the visitors stay behind, but I can't understand how they could keep prisoners here. Those from Conning Square, and your man and Catlin. They surely wouldn't *kill* them."

"That's what we're going to find out," Rollison said.

"Yes," agreed Grice. "We want your watchmen to behave normally. We'll have two of our men in each of the halls, hiding behind the tableaux or the curtains, so that we'll know exactly what they're up to. That's if you're right about the whole thing."

"Are you going to bet?" asked Rollison.

"Not against you," said Grice. "The odds are never long enough."

The last sound of shuffling footsteps and marvelling voices had gone, and the lofty halls were in near-darkness and near-silence. Rollison was with one of Grice's men, in a corner of the Hall of Kings, standing still and trying to breathe without making a sound.

Now and again there was rustling.

Now and again there seemed to be a whisper of voices.

Suddenly, Rollison saw a dark figure of a man against the dim light. The man moved quickly towards the group near Queen Elizabeth the First. He had a torch, which shed a beam of light about the waxen figures. Then he switched the light off, but did not move away. Rollison could just discern him as he stood by one of the figures, and as his eyes became more accustomed to the gloom he saw that the man was pulling the clothes of a figure away from the neck. Soon, the man lifted the head off the actual body. There was a click, followed by a silence which grew almost unbearable, until Grice's man whispered: "Now's the time."

"Right."

The detective put a whistle to his lips, and it shrilled out. Almost as soon as the blast died away, light began to come on, high in the ceiling. The man by the figure of Elizabeth the First stood as if petrified.

It was Wilberforce-Lee.

He held the head upside down, close against his chest, his right hand was actually inside it. He stared towards the Yard men who went briskly towards him. Other detectives came running in from the outer halls, Grice among them. Wilberforce-Lee began to back away, still clutching the head against his chest.

"Don't come near," he said in a reedy voice. "Don't come near."

"Don't waste your time or ours," said Grice, but he did not go too close to the man. "If you give us any trouble you will only make things worse for yourself."

"Keep away," Wilberforce repeated. "If you touch me, I'll—" he broke off.

"There are twenty C.I.D. men in the Exhibition and a dozen others. You haven't a chance to get away," said Grice. "Put that head down, and come with me."

Wilberforce-Lee asked in that reedy voice: "Is Rollison here?"

"I'm here," called Rollison.

"Make Grice understand." said Wilberforce-Lee. "If he arrests me, you won't see Jolly again—or Catlin—or those girls. You'll never see them again."

Grice said: "We don't frighten so easily."

"You'd better," the man said, shrilly. "I knew you

might cotton onto this sooner or later, but—" he broke off, looking at Rollison. "I thought you'd have the sense to handle it yourself. I didn't think you'd bring the police. Tell them I mean it. You won't see Jolly or Catlin or those girls alive unless you let me go." He was backing away all the time, obviously scared, obviously serious. "I'm the only man alive who knows where they are."

"Are they alive?" Rollison asked.

"They are *now*. They won't be for long, unless you make the police let me go."

"Where are they?" asked Grice. It sounded what it was, an empty question.

"Let me go, and I'll tell you," Wilberforce-Lee promised. Then suddenly he screamed at the top of his voice: "Daffodil! Look out."

Only Rollison kept looking at him, all the others swung round as if to see Daffodil. Wilberforce flung the head of Elizabeth I at Rollison, and as Rollison dodged, the man cried again:

"Daffodil! Get away!"

The head crashed onto the floor in the hall itself. Wilberforce-Lee flung his arms out, and a dozen little objects hurtled through the air, falling among the statues and bursting into flame. The figure of Lady Jane Grey began to burn, and flames began to leap up the robes of Mary Queen of Scots, another fire started in the hair of Charles I. As the flames spurted and crackled, Grice's men and the night-watchmen began to put them out. Ebbutt's voice reached an all time high as he roared:

"Extinguishers! Get the fire extinguishers!"

Rollison was darting in Wilberforce-Lee's wake, between the statues. One went flying as the man pushed past it. Two men closed on Wilberforce-Lee as he flung some of the little incendiaries in front of them, making them jump out of his way. Rollison was still some distance away from him.

Wilberforce-Lee reached the exit to the landing.

A dozen men were like a solid phalanx on the stairs, moving with military precision. There was no way of scattering them, no way of escape. The man swung round. Rollison was only a few yards behind him, and he saw the man's hands were empty, so there was no danger of more incendiaries.

He said: "Give it up, or—"

Wilberforce-Lee swung round and vaulted the railing,

trying to get behind the policemen coming up the stairs.
Instead, he missed his grip, slipped, and fell headlong. No
one could save him, no one could help him.

He struck the stone steps of the lower flight head first.

"He died instantaneously," a Yard man said, in 'a dry
voice. "Went out like a light."

"The only one who can help us now is Daffodil Lee,"
Grice said. "She's not here—he called out as if she was
so as to fool us."

"There's no one else in the place—no one except our
men and Rollison's friends," said Fox, who was here too.
"We've searched every room, every cupboard, every possible hiding place."

"Except about five hundred," Rollison remarked.

Grice frowned. "If that's supposed to be funny—"

"Not funny," Rollison assured him. "We know there was
a battery in the head that Wilberforce-Lee had, that it
had softened the wax inside, so that if anything had been
hidden in it he could have got it out. Nothing was hidden,
but he was sure something is hidden in some of the heads.
Obviously he was looking for diamonds. Perfect hiding
place," he added almost admiringly. "Warm the inside of
a wax head, press in diamonds—press in anything small
for that matter—and then smear some wax over the diamonds. They wouldn't be found in a hundred years. First
check the bodies, to make sure the costumes aren't cov-
ering dead or unconscious people, and incidentally, check
the heads."

Ebbutt, standing near Rollison, asked in a wheezy whisper:

"Do you think he might have covered their *faces* in
wax? Suffocate 'em, that would."

"We're going to find out," Rollison said.

Grice was already detailing men to the various halls,
Bernard Tussaud went to one hall with his night-watchmen, Rollison went downstairs with Ebbutt and his men.
As they approached the Chamber of Horrors, more policemen came in from the street, the place seemed nearly
as crowded as by day.

One after another, the figures were checked. Figure
after figure was moved, each head lifted off cautiously,
the dummy body poked and prodded. Upstairs, men were
doing the same thing among the stage and screen stars.
Charlie Chaplin was as ridiculous as the comedian had

ever looked, Diana Dors 'as seductive, Julie Andrews as fragile, Frankie Vaughan as gay. Among the sportsmen and women Sonny Liston looked as enormous as he was, Stirling Moss as bold, Johnny Haynes as thoughtful—

Suddenly, 'a policeman cried: "Here's a body!"

Beneath the head of an actress of yesterday was another head, adorned with a little grey hair. They took the clothes off, gently, and found the body of Jolly, partly huddled in a box. As word was flashed down to Rollison and he came running, there was another cry, from the Hall of Kings.

"Here's one of the girls!"

"*Look!*" cried Bernard Tussaud. "There's Jim Catlin."

The awful question in all their minds was whether the victims were dead or alive.

They *looked* dead—

CHAPTER 21

HIDING PLACE

ROLLISON took his man's wrist firmly, and felt for the pulse. Grice watched, knowing exactly how he felt. Jolly's eyes and lips were closed, and he did not seem to be breathing. He was fully dressed except for his shoes, but his collar and waistband had been loosened.

Rollison felt a faint beating.

"Well?" asked Grice.

"Drugged, I think," said Rollison in a husky voice, and added: "Drugged, I hope. When the hell are those ambulances coming?"

"They should be here now," Grice said. "Try to take it easy. I'll go and find out if they're waiting."

Rollison stood by Jolly's side while a dozen people moved 'about, or stopped to stare at him, but no one came near. There was a stench of burning and of wax, and of the foam which had put the fires out and kept them to a minimum. The victims had all been found, and were stretched out on the floor, waiting. The ambulance men came hurrying. The four girls were lifted gently, and taken away; then Jolly and Catlin were removed, all were drugged, and perhaps near death.

"What you want is something to do," said Grice to Rol-

lison. "Let's go and search those heads. A dozen have
little bumps inside which may be caused by diamonds
buried in the wax." They went to a long trestle table on
which stood a dozen heads; Bernard Tussaud was with
them, feeling inside the cavity with his sensitive fingers.

"It could be done, quite easily. All the hair is sham-
pooed and the faces washed, regularly. A skilled artisan
such as Wilberforce-Lee could easily hide small stones
this way, there would be no difficulty about it. I—ah!"

He broke off, and looked up at Grice sharply.

"There's something hard in here," he said. "I've
scratched the wax, and caught something on my nail.
Wait." They stood almost with bated breath as he flicked
a lighter, held it inside the head to soften the wax, and
then took the flame away. Soon he put his hand inside the
head. When he withdrew it there was a small object between his thumb and forefinger.

Grice took it, and rubbed the wax off.

"It's just a stone," Bernard said, in disappointment.

"So is an uncut diamond," said Rollison. "Well, Bill?"

"I'd say a diamond," Grice answered. "Are there any
more in there, Mr. Tussaud?"

There were nine more diamonds in that head, twenty-
eight more in another, altogether nearly a hundred 'stones'
were found, and if in fact they were diamonds, each was
worth a thousand pounds or more.

Each could be worth a million, for all Rollison cared.
His only serious thought was for Jolly.

Jolly was in a drugged coma, but his breathing was
better.

All four of Daffodil Lee's girl friends were improving,
too, and so was Catlin.

It was now only a matter of waiting for them to come
round and tell what had happened—and perhaps to tell
the police where they might find Daffodil Lee.

For Daffodil was still missing, and despite a nationwide
hunt and her photograph in every newspaper and all the
television channels, there was no news of her.

But there was news of Jolly, twenty-four hours after he
had been found. He recovered consciousness, and was
soon able to talk.

"I am afraid it was my own fault, and due to my own
carelessness," Jolly said. "I went to the studio in Conning
Square, to talk to the young ladies, but none of them was

there. I began to search the studio, and was caught by the man Wilberforce, whom you now tell me is Daffodil Lee's father. He simply struck me with a weighted cosh. Since that time I have been completely oblivious. I should have been much more careful," Jolly finished bitterly, "I cannot give you any help at all, I'm afraid."

"I'll tell you when to start blaming yourself," said Rollison. "Take it easy here for a few days. The Wrightsons are doing quite nicely."

Soon, he was with Grice and Catlin, who had also come round.

"My own fault," Catlin growled. "I didn't trust Wilberforce, but didn't say anything to you about it. I wanted to cover myself with glory by out-Toffing the Toff. I knew Wilberforce lived at Conning Square, and went there and accused him of causing the trouble. He damaged my head," Catlin finished ruefully. "The next thing I knew was waking up here. How are those four girls?"

Liz Bonham was the spokesman for the four girl artists, who were in a four-bed ward in the hospital.

"We couldn't really understand Daffodil," Liz said, "but we believed her when she told us that because of you, her engagement had been broken off and all she wanted was to get her own back on you. She said that damaging the model of your head was a joke, and in a way it was. But then one of us—Isobel, as a matter of fact—came back to the studio early one day, and heard her talking to Wilberforce, whom we knew sometimes lived down in the basement. She was saying that he would have to get rid of Philip Gant, because Philip knew the truth about some diamonds, and that there were diamonds hidden somewhere at Madame Tussaud's. Isobel came upstairs and told the rest of us, and Wilberforce crept after her. Daffodil actually gave us each an injection while the man stood over us. The next thing we knew, we came round here."

"Did you hear anything more about Philip Gant?" asked Rollison.

"Yes, a bit. He was desperately in love with Daffodil, we all knew that. Poor, poor Philip," Liz said softly. "I don't think any of us realised how he felt. I don't know what he would have done if he had discovered that Daffodil was married."

"The *bitch!*" exclaimed dark-haired Isobel, with great intensity.

"To whom?" asked Rollison.

"We didn't get any further than that—Is heard Daffodil talking to Wilberforce, and then they broke off. Is came up to tell us, and you know what happened after that."

"You must find her," Is Allington cried.

"The remarkable thing is that there have been practically no reports about her—not one tenth as many as I'd expected after all the publicity," Grice said. "She seems to have vanished off the face of the earth. Have you any idea at all, Rolly?"

"No," Rollison said, "Except—"

"Ah."

"I'd like to go down to Southampton and see the Frankens off," Rollison said. "My way of making some kind of amends. And it's just possible that they'll remember something Daffodil said, or some place she often went to. I'll try to jog their memory, anyhow. Any suggestions?"

"You feel almost guilty about them, don't you?" said Grice. "Their parents were murderers, you know. And we've now got enough evidence to prove that the parents worked with King, Wilberforce-Lee and Daffodil. So they were a pretty bad lot."

The *Matopas Castle* was due to sail in half an hour when Rollison reached the dockside at half-past three the following afternoon. The hatches were down, and some visitors were actually coming off the ship when Rollison went on board. A loud-speaker boomed and a man called over it:

"All visitors ashore, please. The ship is ready to sail."

An official of the line escorted Rollison to the Cabin Class on 'B' deck, and went along to B71, the double cabin which Ethel Franken was sharing. Her brothers were only two cabins away, in B75. The official knocked on the door, and a woman called out:

"Who's that?"

"Your steward, Miss."

"All right, just a minute," called the woman. In less than a minute the door opened, while she went on: "What is it? I asked not to be disturbed."

Then she stopped, open-mouthed.

Her hair was glossy black, she wore a tailored suit, and no one who noticed her in passing would dream that she was a natural blonde. But she had Daffodil's height and Daffodil's eyes, and suddenly she flew into a Daffodil rage. This time, Rollison was fully prepared, and he grabbed her arms before she could scratch or bite.

"Now we'll get the Frankens," Rollison said. "And we'll telephone the police."

The police came from Southampton, searched the cabin, and found as many diamonds as there had been buried in wax at Madame Tussaud's.

It was late that evening when Rollison saw Grice, in the Gresham Terrace flat. By then, Daffodil and all the Frankens were in Cannon Row, awaiting a charge and a hearing next morning. Grice, relaxed and even half-amused, sat back in an easy chair.

"So you didn't feel guilty about the Frankens," he said wryly.

"Hardly," said the Toff. "They protested their innocence far too much, even if convincingly. I didn't believe Wilberforce-Lee got in and out of their house without their knowledge. And I'd come to the conclusion that when frightened, Daffodil was simply herself. When she was in a jam she blamed them, hoping they would be able to get out of trouble. Daffodil is a psychopath, of course."

"Two doctors have now agreed on that," said Grice. "It was pretty obvious when she pitched into you. We've found sleeping tablets in the lining of her handbags, too— she kept dosing herself, so as to be able to blame you for doping her. How she hates you!"

"And she could never hide it. I was at the root of all her troubles, and she couldn't conceal her feelings even though she knew she was making me wonder what it was all about. But why she went so far as to damage my wax head and the photograph—"

Rollison broke off, for Grice stared at him incredulously. After a pause, Rollison was piqued into saying:

"Now what?"

"You mean you think Daffodil did that?"

"Didn't she?" asked Rollison blankly. "Then who—"

He broke off, as understanding began to dawn, but it did not shine brightly until Grice said in a puzzled voice:

"I thought you knew. Philip Gant did the damage. Philip knew how his beloved hated you. He followed her everywhere, and no one took any notice of him. He had her keys. He knew exactly what she was planning, that was why he was murdered before you could get to him, and make him talk. Gant was going blind, and to him the most vulnerable spot was an eye. It was to counteract much of the effect of what he did that the four friends of Daffodil were brought in. They made it all seem like a gigantic hoax, to stall you until the diamonds were found."

"Well, well," Rollison said faintly.

"Don't be despondent," Grice said. "You did make a bee-line for the Frankens. If you hadn't we would probably never have caught them or Daffodil."

"Some consolation," muttered Rollison. "But Philip Gant—oh, well. At least I wondered about Daffodil and Wilberforce when they came to my flat. She couldn't hide her dislike, and Wilberforce was obviously afraid she would say too much. At the time it wasn't important but it took on significance later. The story would probably never have come out if Madame Tussaud's hadn't decided to put my model in. My well-known reputation as a private detective made Wilberforce and all the others fear that I'd been asked to look for the diamonds. You assumed I was after evidence against the young Frankens, remember. Wilberforce couldn't believe I was simply to be featured at the Exhibition. Can't say I blame him."

Two weeks later, Rollison and Jolly, Norah and Isobel, Mandy and Liz, all of Ebbutt's men who had helped in the case, and also Superintendent William Grice, were guests at a little ceremony at Madame Tussaud's. A new tableaux was being opened in the Chamber of Horrors, and champagne was to flow. Bernard Tussaud and his brother, Eva, Catlin, Ebbutt and several of his men, were there to see the figure of the Toff installed, facing the Franken parents in the small alcove.

"Let's hear from you, Toff!"

"Speech!"

The Toff held up a hand. A dozen still cameras flashed and a television camera began to whirr.

"All we need for today is a figure of speech," said the Toff, and as they shouted him down, he was smiling . . .

He was still smiling, sometime later, when he placed a piece of beeswax on a glass slide, pressed a piece of broken shoe-lace into it, and placed these together on a small stand on the Trophy Wall. As he watched him, Jolly said mildly:

"That certainly makes quite an impression, sir."